'Twas the w[...]
Ninetee[...]
The season's joy overshadowed
by the war just begun.

———————

The Great Depression years finally behind them, the entire Coleman family of Pittsburgh has been looking forward to this Christmas for almost the entire year. For the first time in more than a decade, Gerald and Irene Coleman have tucked away enough extra money to make up for all the lean years of disappointingly modest Christmas gifts for their children.

But December 7, 1941 has changed everything, and for the past two weeks the entire family has followed with despair the Japanese advances all over the Pacific as well as America finally being dragged into the two-year old European war. A few glimmers of hope can be found in the war news, but both parents fear not only for the country's fate as this new war begins but, more personally, for the fate of their sons who will likely soon be joining the fighting in one war theater or another.

Still, despite the sense of dread hanging over almost every aspect of the family's daily affairs, Irene Coleman is determined that if indeed this will be the last Christmas that the family spends together—at least until after the war, or perhaps even forever—then she will do everything in her power to make Christmas, 1941, the first Christmas of the war, a happy one for her children and her entire family.

Come spend the week leading up to Christmas, 1941 with the Coleman family:

Jonathan—The eldest son at nineteen, Jonathan fatalistically realizes the inevitability of his military days arriving very soon, whether he succumbs to the pressure to enlist or if he waits until he is drafted. But Jonathan has other problems on his mind as well. His long-time girlfriend Francine Donner, whom only days from now he plans to ask to marry him, broke a date with him this past weekend to go out with Donnie Yablonski, one of Jonathan's best friends from high school (and one of her own former boyfriends before Jonathan), because Donnie is headed off to boot camp right after Christmas. Jonathan has ominous feelings about this turn of events... and he's right.

Joseph—At seventeen years old, Joseph has been acting like a walking recruiting poster ever since the Pearl Harbor attack, constantly talking about how he can't wait to "join up and see action." Spurred on by his cousin during a family post-church Sunday brunch, Joseph's one-track behavior goes into overdrive in the days leading up to Christmas, causing increasing strife and contention with his more reticent older brother and with his parents.

Charlene—The third child in the family and the oldest daughter, Charlene has just become secretly engaged at the age of sixteen to her boyfriend who is soon headed to boot camp. She shares the news of her engagement with her cousin Lorraine Walker, but Lorraine quickly breaks her promise to keep the news secret. When Irene Coleman learns of her daughter's engagement and the circumstances surrounding it, she has yet another problem to confront.

Thomas—With the new war and the family tensions involving his brothers and his older sister, plus a general feeling of uneasiness, fourteen-year old Thomas' shift from childhood to his teenage years is becoming more and more unsettled each day. Throughout his childhood, he had looked forward to Christmas each year, even though his haul of toys was, like each of his siblings', meager during the Depression years. This year, though, Thomas can't wait until Christmas is over, feeling that any kind of holiday celebration is out of place given the times.

Ruth—Six-year old Ruth doesn't fully comprehend the magnitude of what is occurring in the world and what has, in the past few weeks, hit every corner of American life. All she cares about is Christmas, and she is particularly upset that the promised family trip to downtown Pittsburgh for Christmas shopping and looking at the window displays is now more than a week overdue.

Gerald—The patriarch of the family, Gerald Coleman has never worked for anybody but himself, being able to hang on to his shoemaker shop—and his family's house—during the Depression years. Now, however, spurred by the trials that his sons will soon face in the Army or Navy, he is considering going to work in one of the war plants springing up in Pittsburgh and all across America to "do his part for the war effort."

Irene—In many ways, the backbone of the family... the classical 1930s-1940s matriarch who runs her household her way, no questions asked. Like her husband, Irene is mortified by the ominous war news and does her best to occupy the hours of her day with an endless string of tasks and chores, trying to keep her mind off her own fears for her sons' safety.

December 20-26, 1941:

The First Christmas of the War

The First Christmas of the War

First Printing 2010
Printed in the United States of America
First Edition

ISBN-10: 0982720890
ISBN-13:978-0-9827208-9-9

Kindle
ISBN-10: 0982720831
ISBN-13: 978-0-9827208-3-7

ePub
ISBN-10: 098272084X
ISBN-13: 978-0-9827208-4-4

PDF
ISBN-10: 0982720858
ISBN-13: 978-0-9827208-5-1

Front cover calendar image compliments and courtesy of The C.E. Daniel Collection/ www.danielsww2.com
Back cover image compliments and courtesy of Snyder's Treasures/ www.snyderstreasures.com

The First Christmas of the War

a novel by Alan Simon

Dedicated to my great-uncles—the real-life sons of "J. Weisberg & Sons" whom I use as minor background characters in this novel, and also my other great-uncles who married into the family during or shortly after the war—who, like millions of other Americans of their generation, sacrificed much of their youth to the Second World War

Prologue—Saturday Morning, December 20, 1941

"My God, I have so much to do today!" was, like on most other mornings, Irene Coleman's first thought of the day as she reached to shut off the alarm bell. Cooking breakfast, dusting and cleaning, the laundry, shopping at the corner market and the butcher shop and the bakery... the list of tasks always seemed endless, and Irene—a natural worrier anyway—fretted as her mind shuffled and reshuffled the list. Even though she allowed herself an extra half hour of sleep on Saturdays—the 6:00 A.M. alarm gave her almost six hours in bed, in contrast to her 5:30 A.M. rising time on weekdays and Sundays—she already felt exhausted as she swung her legs over the side of the bed and her feet fished on the chilled oak plank floor for her slippers. Throughout this past night, like many other nights, her dreams had been dominated by the same chores and responsibilities that filled her days, making Irene feel that her life was one endless series of 24-hour work cycles without pause.

No rest for the weary, Irene thought to herself as she grabbed her threadbare bathrobe from the back of the bedroom door. Maybe Gerald will buy me a new bathrobe for Christmas this year, she thought, looking back to the bed through the darkness at the outline of her still sleeping husband; I certainly could use one, the faded one she was now draping over her nightgown having seen more than a decade's service.

After a brief stop in the chilly bathroom Irene headed down the stairs to the kitchen, flicking on the ceiling light and silently grousing about the darkness at this time of year. At the first signs of daylight an hour from now she would shut off the overhead light—no sense in wasting electricity and, more importantly, money—and get by for the rest of the day on whatever natural light God saw fit to bestow on Pittsburgh that day. Last night's weather forecast for today had indicated overcast skies with a threat of snow throughout the day, so Irene knew that bright streaming daylight wasn't in the picture for this morning, or later in the day as she made her way around the neighborhood. Tomorrow was Sunday, so today she needed to visit the market, the bakery, and the butcher since all of those places would be closed tomorrow. Irene would be bundled up against the cold, but some bright daylight as she made her rounds would certainly be welcome; maybe the forecast would be wrong.

Even as she began grinding the coffee beans her mind continued to whirl, arranging and rearranging the sequence of what needed to be done this day. The bakery last instead of first, she now thought, and then maybe the butcher with the market last. Or maybe do the shopping in the morning and the housework in the afternoon, rather than the reverse order she now had planned.

Deep inside the recesses of her mind, Irene Coleman knew that part of the reason she spent so much time lately worrying about her tasks and chores day and night was that doing so kept her mind off of what really worried her... what she really feared. But as she crossed through the living room and opened the front door to retrieve the newspaper and the milkman's delivery, the headline on the morning's *Pittsburgh Post-Gazette*, sitting squarely face-up on the welcome mat right in front of the door brought those fears front and center.

Japs Continue Move on Philippines
Land on Mindanao; Yanks Flee to Hills
Jap Naval Guns Cut Down Filipino Defenses

All in all, Irene Coleman would much rather fret over the drudgery of chores and housework than fear for the safety of her two sons who would soon be thrust into combat in either the Pacific or Europe, most likely followed by their younger brother several years later when he came of age... assuming America could hold on in the war that long.

She forced her eyes away from the newspaper's ominous headline, looking instead towards the tin milk box. She opened the box and pulled out the contents that had been delivered about a half hour earlier: the daily delivery of milk and cream—daily except for Sunday, of course—and the twice weekly delivery of cheese and butter that came on Wednesdays and Saturdays. Picking up the butter, she again wondered if the rumors were true, that butter would soon be in very short supply as a result of government-imposed food rationing. Irene had never tasted oleomargarine—even though during the Great War oleo had gained popularity amidst shortages of dairy products—but the few people she knew who had actually tried it were unanimous in their intense dislike for oleo, pronouncing the substance as far inferior to real dairy butter.

Nevertheless, stories of upcoming rationing of not only food but gasoline, various types of metals, and heaven knows what else did nothing to settle Irene's uneasiness that this still-new war would have far-reaching effects on all of their lives, even those who never set foot on a battlefield in Europe or the Pacific.

As Irene turned back towards the house, the newspaper tucked under her left arm and the bottles of milk and cream cradled in the crook of her other arm, the morning's iciness finally hit her. She looked back across the Coleman home's porch across the columns to the small front yard and into the street beyond. Just beneath the porch roof she could see the first swirling of snowflakes in the darkness, and she shook her head. The forecast had been correct about the snow, and if the flurries didn't stop the resulting deposit on the sidewalks would no doubt impede her rounds to the various stores later this morning... or perhaps this afternoon, her mind shifting back into rearranging the day's schedule once again, her eyes refusing to look further to see what other terrible information awaited her in the newsprint.

After shutting the front door she crossed back to the kitchen, dropping the *Post-Gazette* on Gerald's easy chair on the way. Gerald hadn't said much about the new war since the day of the attack on Hawaii—two weeks ago tomorrow, Irene suddenly thought to herself—but he closely followed the war news, reading the paper cover to cover each day. When he did say anything it seemed to Irene that her husband was desperately trying to seek out any bit of war news that could possibly be construed as hopeful. The Russians seemed to have stopped the Germans outside of Moscow—at least for this winter—he had pointed out to Irene and Joseph, at seventeen their second oldest; maybe the Wehrmacht wasn't so invincible after all, despite how easily they had rolled through and conquered continental Europe. And in North Africa, the British were also giving the Germans a battle.

But Gerald Coleman steered clear of any discussion of the new war in the Pacific. What was the sense in talking about Pearl Harbor, Wake Island, the Philippines, Singapore, Malaysia, Guam, and all the rest, where the Japanese seemed unstoppable?

Irene struck a match and lit the stove's pilot light, the "poof" causing her to involuntarily lean backwards as always. She put the two bottles of milk in the icebox to keep the milk cold until breakfast—still more than an hour away—and also stashed the cheese in the icebox but Irene left the cream sit out, since it was only going into the hot coffee anyway, along with the butter that would soften. She gathered what she needed for breakfast—eggs, bacon, potatoes, bread, and bowls and utensils—and began this part of the morning ritual. Even throughout the dark years of the 1930s, when so much of Pittsburgh had been gripped by the Depression just like the rest of the country, Irene Coleman had never failed to start her family's day off with a hearty breakfast of eggs, bacon or ham or sausage, potatoes, toast and butter, and plenty of coffee or milk to drink. Or, for a change on other days, heaps of hotcakes instead of eggs and potatoes.

The Coleman family had been fortunate that Gerald's chosen profession was that of a cobbler, and since few people could afford to buy new shoes in those tight times they would get the same pairs of shoes repaired over and over and over. Gerald Coleman was one of only two cobblers in their mid-Pittsburgh neighborhood, and was almost universally acknowledged as the better of the two.

Gerald's restitching work lasted longer, his replacement soles and heels wore more slowly and evenly, and—most importantly—the prices Gerald charged were very fair. Gerald Coleman even extended credit to select neighbors who were particularly down on their fortunes and almost always was repaid, even up to a year later, when that customer finally found work and scraped together an extra dollar or two. This generosity and empathy earned him the loyalty of most of those in the neighborhood, and even though the Coleman family was hardly flush during those years, by the standards of the times they were at least comfortable and secure. They had been able to keep their house, even though a few years still remained on the mortgage when the Depression began. Gerald Coleman had sworn that come hell or high water—or both—that mortgage *would* be paid off, that the Coleman family would *not* lose their home. And true to his word, the last monthly mortgage payment of $39.53 was made in July, 1935... and with the end of the Depression still nowhere in sight, everyone in the Coleman family, even the children who barely understood what a mortgage was, breathed a bit easier, ten years of monthly payments now behind them and a home worth around $4,500 now in their name, untouchable by the bank.

During those years, one of the few bright spots for the Coleman family— the oldest four children in particular, then all five children after the youngest daughter Ruth was born in 1935—was Christmas. Presents were scarce but never absent. Every year, each child received one or two small inexpensive toys along with an item or two of new clothing. Gerald and Irene began putting money away for Christmas each year in January, almost immediately following the previous year's Christmas, and by the time December rolled around enough had been stashed away to cover presents for the children and a small token gift for each parent.

To the Coleman family, though, Christmas was traditionally more of a seasonal experience, a two- or three-week respite from the troubles of the times, than a one-day distribution of gifts. Each year, Gerald and Irene would take the children downtown one or two nights in mid-December to walk around in the nippy weather and gaze longingly at the department stores' Christmas window displays. The children would good-naturedly argue about whose displays were best each year and cast their respective votes for Kaufmann's or Gimbel's or Horne's, depending on which coveted (though most likely unattainable) goods caught which child's attention that year. Gerald and Irene would carefully note the items in which each child expressed particular interest, and would then purchase a carefully constructed portfolio of as many of those items as feasible over the next week, the hope being that enough of each child's wishes would be satiated to create a memorable holiday season. And then, the hope that next year's Christmas would be better for all...

"Next year" finally came in 1940. The war in Europe, and the resulting Lend-Lease programs to arm England and the Soviet Union to help those nations fight Germany, had resulted in a dramatic increase in demand for steel from the United States. And as steel went, so went Pittsburgh. Even though the overall American economic landscape was still mostly stagnant, with pockets of hope only just beginning to take hold, Pittsburgh and other northern steel towns such as Cleveland and Bethlehem and

Gary, Indiana led the way towards recovery as stagnant steel mills came sputtering back to life. And, as those steel mills began to work around the clock and long-idled steel workers shuffled back to jobs they had finally resigned themselves to being lost forever, the economy in Pittsburgh and those other towns began to pick up as well. People were still cautious enough, though, and even as those who hadn't had a new pair of shoes in years finally indulged, they kept their old pairs in good repair as just-in-case backups, or gave those old shoes to those who were yet less fortunate. Gerald Coleman's shoe repair business still remained prosperous (by the terms of the times) even as economic hope flickered, and because Gerald declined to raise his prices his shoe repair business and the resulting shop profits actually picked up throughout the year.

Presents for the five Coleman children were a bit more generous during Christmas, 1940—but just a bit, though—and as Pittsburgh's economy picked up steam throughout 1941 in lockstep with the pace of hostilities across Europe, Gerald and Irene Coleman thought that 1941 would finally be the year that long-coveted gifts could finally be purchased for their children: baseball gloves and bats for the boys, dolls for the girls, bicycles for all...

The Japanese attack on Pearl Harbor and the declarations of war across the globe that followed changed all that, though. Nothing had changed economically—the money that had been saved up all year by Gerald and Irene, enough money for every child to have a bike and several other presents, was still safely stashed away—but with the uncertainty of what lay ahead, neither parent felt comfortable splurging on the so-long-delayed deluge of Christmas presents that had been planned only weeks earlier. And just like that, hoarding savings and minimizing spending was once again of paramount importance.

Still, Irene Coleman wanted this Christmas to be a special one for the family, extravagant presents or not. She knew that by next year's Christmas nineteen-year old Jonathan—the oldest—would be wearing one type of military uniform or another, and might very well be engaged in combat on Christmas Day itself... if he hadn't already been killed or wounded. Joseph, the second oldest at 17, will have turned 18 and given the boy's nonstop chatter about not being able to wait to join the Army or the Marines, will certainly have enlisted by then. She had even overheard Joseph tell Gerald that he wanted to drop out of high school and enlist, but at 17 he needed his father's permission and signature, and Irene had heard Gerald tersely tell the boy that he didn't want to hear another word about it, that Joseph would be in the military soon enough and that there was no way he'd condone his son dropping out of high school to enlist. Gerald hadn't mentioned a word of this conversation to his wife, which told Irene that her husband was troubled by all aspects of that exchange with his second oldest son.

The two oldest boys would certainly be gone by next Christmas, which would leave the other three children: their daughter Charlene, who would then be 17; their third son, Thomas, who would be 15; and the youngest child, Ruth, who would then be seven. Three children at home would be better than none, of course, but Irene Coleman did her best to fight off the sadness that threatened to envelop her when she thought that one year from now, the other two would not only be gone but might be facing imminent danger and, indeed, may even have fallen victim to that danger.

So far this year, Gerald and Irene hadn't taken the children downtown for the annual walking and shopping ritual because of the war-caused confusion and the time needed for home defense preparations: organizing neighborhood civil defense and air watch patrols, sewing and fitting blackout curtains for all the windows, and stocking the basement with emergency sleeping and eating provisions. That omission would be rectified this coming Monday evening, though, with the delayed downtown trip. All the children, even the oldest sons who seemed to be outgrowing the family ritual the previous year, anxiously awaited the family trip and had been pestering their parents for this much-needed diversion and semblance of normalcy.

And so Irene Coleman vowed to herself that despite everything—the turmoil and confusion of the past two weeks, the fear and uncertainty of what lay ahead—this year's Christmas, the first Christmas of the war and quite possibly the last Christmas that all of the seven Coleman family members would ever be together on that day, would be a special and memorable one for all of them.

Irene heard heavy footsteps on the stairs, and knew without looking that Gerald was descending, as he did most Saturday mornings, five or ten minutes after she did. For Gerald Coleman, Saturday was like any other workday—any day other than Sunday—and she knew his routine by heart: a grunted "g'mornin'" to his wife as he looked towards the kitchen doorway the same instant she would walk there to look towards the stairway, followed by a scan of the *Post-Gazette's* headlines and then a stroll out to the front porch to get a first-hand appraisal of this morning's weather, the weather through which he would walk the four blocks to his little store to be open by 7:15 that morning.

The children would soon be following him down the stairs, Irene thought to herself as she forced her thoughts back to the morning's breakfast and yet another mental pass through her obligations for the day... anything except thinking about the meaning of the headlines in the paper at which Gerald Coleman was now staring, slowly shaking his head with sorrow and worry.

1—Sunday, December 21, 1941

Like every other father of military-age sons in St. Michael's Church this Sunday morning—or in any other church, Catholic or otherwise, across all of Pittsburgh and throughout America—Gerald Coleman prayed for the safety of his sons when their inevitable military service began. Whether Jonathan and Joseph—and probably even Thomas, since the war would no doubt last long enough for his now-14-year old son to be dragged into it—wound up in the Army or the Navy or the Marines, or perhaps the Air Corps, they would likely be in serious danger for years, given how the war had gone so far.

The war: horrifying, depressing news, not only the recent events— the endless Japanese attacks against American and British forces all over the Pacific over the past two weeks— but over in Europe and North Africa for more than two years now. Whether his sons faced the Japs or the Germans, they would be in for the fight of their lives, given the staggering might of each of those enemies' forces.

But in addition to praying for his sons' well-being, Gerald Coleman also prayed for forgiveness... for himself. When the boys were growing up Gerald often told them tales of his own time in the Army during the Great War. Like so many young men born just before the turn of the century, Gerald Coleman had gone Over There when America entered the European war in 1917. But unlike the hundreds of thousands who spent the war in the trenches, facing fixed bayonet charges and dawning gas masks on a moment's notice in the face of mustard gas attacks, Gerald spent his seven months on the continent in a rear echelon supply unit, never coming closer than twenty miles from the enemy the entire time he was there. After the armistice, Gerald Coleman came back to America to resume his apprenticeship to his shoemaker father, cementing the path of his life that carried through to this day.

But as his sons were growing up, Gerald regaled them with tales of his own days in the Army. Never having seen combat he saw no reason to tell them nail-biting stories about bayonet charges or gas attacks or any of the other horrors he hadn't actually experienced. He not only wouldn't fabricate tales of his own heroism that had never happened, he also knew enough about what his comrades had gone through not to glorify combat.

Still, Gerald's tales of Army days gaiety and mischief provided (he thought, anyway) diversion to his sons amidst the daily dreariness and constant worry of those Depression years. Throughout the 1930s, sitting on the family home porch on summer evenings or gathered around the fireplace on winter nights, Gerald would frequently tell his sons the story of his flight one day in the back seat of Eddie Rickenbacker's biplane to deliver a box of ammunition and a top secret communiqué to a battalion commander who, it turns out, reported directly to General Pershing. Then there was the time when Gerald and two other buddies swiped three horses from the cavalry's stable, rode several miles to a farmhouse they had spotted a week earlier in the French countryside, and had a picnic with three French sisters. (He of course left out the details of his very first sexual experience that same day with one of those sisters in the barn's hayloft, but even with that omission Gerald had told his oldest sons conspiratorially "... and don't tell your mother anything about this" when he finally added this tale to the repertoire only a couple of years earlier.)

Gerald did his best to make a stint in the military seem like a highly desirable and memorable interlude for a young man before his life's journey (the unspoken word: drudgery) began. Jonathan, his oldest son, initially seemed enthralled by these stories but over the past two years, as war gripped Europe courtesy of the Wehrmacht and the Luftwaffe, and U-boats ravaged shipping all over the Atlantic, he grew increasingly quiet—almost moody—as if he somehow sensed that the day would soon be here when he'd know firsthand that his father's tales of "Fun in the Army" were nowhere near as enjoyable as his father made it all sound.

The second-oldest, however, was a walking recruiting poster for military service. For the past two years, Joseph had often talked about learning to fly airplanes and one day joining the Flying Tigers in China or the Eagle Squadron in England, shooting down Japs or Germans and getting his picture on the cover of *Life* after he became an ace. Or if flying was out of the question (money for flight lessons being nowhere in the picture, of course), maybe enlisting in the Marines as soon as he turned 18 with the intention that he would spend a couple of years frolicking on the beaches of the Hawaiian Islands, creating his own set of adventures that he would someday tell to his own sons.

Whereas the attack on Pearl Harbor had sent Jonathan into a deep funk—the clock was now ticking very loudly, and Jonathan knew it was only a matter of months until he was wearing one type of uniform or another—Joseph seemed to feed on the war frenzy, and his chatter about his own inevitable military service became nonstop and even more gleeful. The war was finally here, Joseph cackled; and though he didn't use these exact words, his father could read his mind: "I'll finally become a man when I face combat."

And so, Gerald Coleman prayed for forgiveness. He didn't want his sons to be so afraid of what they would have to do that they would not be able to do their part in defending America against these threats, but at the same time he couldn't shake the feeling that Joseph's eagerness—an eagerness unquestionably fed by Gerald's stories—was a bad omen for the boy.

Gerald leaned slightly forward and looked across Irene, sitting to his right (Gerald occupied his customary aisle seat on the right side of the church's bank of pews, near the front of the church), at his children who were lined up next to their mother, youngest to oldest. Ruth, the youngest, angel-faced with her blond shoulder-length curly hair, sitting there in her homemade dark brown dress, no doubt worrying about whether the war—whatever "war" was, at her age she probably didn't fully comprehend what was happening—would ruin Christmas. Thomas, just arriving at that awkward, gawky age when his boyish face was starting to evolve into the man's face it would become, his head moving slightly as his eyes lazily swept across the statues of the saints and stained glass windows, most likely daydreaming or doing anything but concentrating on the prayers and hymns laid out in the book resting on his lap.

Sixteen-year old Charlene, sitting to Thomas' right, probably thinking about Larry Moncheck, her seventeen-year old boyfriend and a classmate of Joseph's, who would soon face the same decisions that Joseph would: finish high school or not; enlist or wait to be drafted; Army or Navy or Marines, or perhaps the Army Air Forces? Gerald's eyes paused on Charlene as he noticed for the very first time how much his daughter looked like her mother had the first time Gerald had noticed Irene when they had both been teenagers, so many years ago: carefully styled shoulder-length light brown hair, the facial beauty that had not only Larry Moncheck but also several other of Joseph's classmates mooning over her... and a hint of some unspoken secret dancing in her brown eyes as she slowly gazed about the church, finally catching her father's eye for a second before he looked away towards his older sons.

Joseph. Sitting next to Charlene, Gerald was fairly certain that his second oldest was fantasizing about battlefield glory, killing scores of Japs or Germans and being greeted upon his return home as a conquering hero. At seventeen, sometimes Joseph still looked like the boy he so recently was, his dark brown hair sweeping down and almost covering his right eye, but other times the first impression Gerald had was of a young man, filling out in face and body, and at only two inches shy of six feet—the same height as his older brother—three inches taller than his own father now.

And finally Jonathan, sitting furthest away from his father, named by his mother after the Old Testament character who had exhibited such bravery and loyalty to the future King David even though doing so put him at odds with his own father. Gerald had wanted to name his first-born John after his own father, but Irene had insisted on the "Jonathan" variation. Gerald had no doubt that Jonathan would, when the time came, exhibit the same courage that he had on the athletic fields at Schenley High

School as the school's star football player for four years, despite usually being one of the shortest and lightest-weight players on the field.

Gerald knew, though, that the boy's mind was troubled, and he wished that Jonathan would talk with his father about exactly what was bothering him; maybe there was some wisdom he could impart to ease his son's mind.

Gerald watched Jonathan sitting there, flipping through his hymnal with a purpose and occasionally stopping to read some passage that he had apparently been seeking. Unlike Joseph's longish, almost unkempt hair, Jonathan had retained the crewcut he had worn while playing on various Schenley teams, and his whitish scalp peeked through the stubs of dark brown hair. Now a year out of high school, his face had lost all remaining traces of boyishness, the aging no doubt helped along by the fatigue of his job down in the Strip District at a produce wholesaler that began at 3:30 every morning and lasted until just after noon.

Irene had insisted that the entire Coleman family go to her brother Stan's house for Sunday dinner after church ended. Ordinarily, they all would walk the seven blocks back home from St. Michael's immediately after the service ended, Irene would fix them a quick dinner shortly after noon, and they would all scatter for their assigned household chores. Afterwards, the children could spend the remaining few hours of daylight playing outside in the small backyard if the weather wasn't too cold. Or, if Irene determined that the weather was too inhospitable for the children to spend time outdoors (and Irene was the only member of the family who would make this determination; even Gerald couldn't overrule his wife if the children wanted to go outside but Irene determined that was not to be so that day), the five Coleman children would wile away those hours playing games or listening to the radio.

But today, they would all be at the home of Stan and Lois Walker and their three children for the afternoon, and Gerald was none too happy about it. After all, he had seen enough of Stan and his family during the almost six years that they had all lived in Gerald's house, years that Stan was out of work and almost always out of money.

The original plans up until two weeks ago had been for the families to spend Christmas Day together at the Walker's house, with Lois preparing an abundant feast as a display of gratitude to Gerald and Irene and their children for the years of hospitality (and plenty of inconvenience, Gerald thought but of course would not say out loud) in those so-dark days for Irene's brother and his family. This past February Stan finally was called back to work to his brakeman job at Penn Central after having been furloughed indefinitely from the railroad in 1935, and with a few dollars finally coming in Stan was able to rent a modest house two streets away from Gerald and Irene.

Following the Pearl Harbor attack and the declarations of war with Germany and Japan that followed, and given the sad realization that when Christmas, 1942 rolled around Jonathan and Joseph would be in some far-off location away from the family, Irene had changed her mind and insisted that the Coleman family spend one last Christmas with the entire family—and only their family—

together. Even after this war was over, whenever that might be, and if her sons survived and came back home, they would be adults—maybe even with families of their own—and future Christmas days would no doubt be different... better, possibly, but certainly different.

And so plans had changed and this coming Thursday the Coleman family would leave church, much as they are doing now, but instead of going to the Walkers' house for the day, they would come back to their own home. But to avoid any hurt feelings, Irene and her sister-in-law agreed that today, the families would have Sunday dinner together with Lois' feast accelerated by several days.

But Gerald Coleman wasn't quite in the mood to listen to his brother-in-law today, and it would take all his willpower to grit his teeth as Stan Walker would no doubt chatter on about how General Motors stock would certainly double by this time next year. Back in the mid- and late 1920s, Stan Walker—only in his twenties then—had, like so many others, become captivated by the roaring stock market that kept going up and up and up. As a railroad brakeman his salary was a modest one, but by 1925 he had begun buying a few shares of RCA, a few more shares of American Can, and by the time the summer of 1929 had rolled around Stan Walker had almost $40,000 worth of stock certificates to his name... a fortune!

"You have to get in on this!" Stan Walker had told his brother-in-law (and anyone else who would listen) time and time again, until the stock market crash in October, 1929 wiped out a third of that forty grand. The rest trickled away over the next couple of years, and by New Year's Day, 1934 it was all gone... every penny. His layoff from the railroad the following year cemented the Walker family's fate, and other than an occasional short-term WPA job no money was coming in at all. The bank took their house in the spring of 1935, and after conferring (pleading) with her husband, Irene opened her home to her brother and his family, not dreaming that almost six years would pass before the arrangement would end.

During those years living under Gerald Coleman's roof, Stan Walker knew better than to discuss what stocks he thought had bottomed out and would be a good buy, if only he could scrape together a couple of extra dollars. But over the past few months, as war enveloped Europe and select industrial cities across America—including Pittsburgh—sputtered back to life (and, one hoped—but dared not mouth the word—*prosperity*), and after Stan Walker moved his family into their own house for the first time in years, he once again began talking about the killing that could be made in the stock market in light of the war and the resulting increased industrial activity. United States Steel; General Motors; Alcoa; Stan's wish list of stocks to buy went on and on. Gerald Coleman only grimaced—but held his tongue—when his brother-in-law started on his "I wish I could buy stocks" routine, but over the past few months that was almost all Stan talked about whenever their families got together or if they happened to pass each other on the street. No doubt Stan would be in full swing this afternoon—Gerald swiveled his head to the left and looked back at where Stan and Lois and their children were sitting, catching Stan absent-mindedly mouthing "The Lord's Prayer," no doubt wondering to himself what the price of Gulf Oil would be come tomorrow morning when the stock market opened. To Gerald's way of thinking, the stock market was for people who lived in New

York City or maybe Chicago. The only people from Pittsburgh who had any business playing the stock market were those with names like Carnegie, Mellon, and Frick... not Coleman or Walker.

❀ ❀ ❀

"Marty, will you please say grace."

Stan Walker's words caused Gerald and Irene Coleman, sitting next to each other at the Walker's dining room table, to imperceptibly shoot glances of amazement mixed with concern at each other. When the Walker family had first moved in with the Coleman's after their former house had been lost to the bank, the four parents had tried to enlist the Walkers' children in the before-meal prayer ritual at every evening supper and any weekend meals the families had together. Martin Walker—Marty to everyone, including his own parents—was the same age as Joseph Coleman, but was far more mischievous and even devilish of a boy when growing up than even impetuous Joseph was. The few times either Stan or Gerald had asked Marty to say grace during those years (before they learned better), the boy's "blessing" was of the "Good food, good meat, good God, let's eat!" variety. While neither Gerald nor Irene was fanatically Catholic, both considered such irreverence when speaking directly to God as a bad omen at the very least, especially in the unsettled times that were the mid-1930s.

Oh well, it's Stan's house, Irene sighed to herself, figuring that her husband was likely thinking an identical thought. So both were surprised when seventeen year old

Martin Louis Walker began with something akin to a traditional grace.

"Heavenly father, we thank you for this bounty before us. We pray that you protect all of us in this time of trouble for our country."

But then came:

"And we pray that Jonathan, Joseph, and I soon have the chance to kill as many Krauts and Japs as possible. Amen!"

The boy's enthusiastic and concluding "Amen!" came before his parents, Gerald, or Irene could react, but each of the four adults just sat there, open-mouthed, incredulous at what they had just heard. Gerald shot a look at his oldest two sons. Jonathan had a look that could only be described as a combination of amazement and fear, but Joseph's eyes were on his cousin and they seemed to blaze alive, a smirk just then coming to his face, silently communicating solidarity with the sentiment Marty had just voiced.

Stan Walker finally found his voice.

"What the hell was that?"

Lois Walker shot her own look at her husband, briefly and temporarily transferring her growing fury away from her son to her husband.

"Watch your language at the table!" she growled at Stan, before turning her attention—and anger—back to her son.

"I *never* want to hear anything like that from you ever again, especially during a blessing over food on our table!" The timbre of her voice remained even, but she left no room for misinterpretation that if she ever heard Martin Walker voice such sentiment again in her presence, he would be extremely sorry.

Irene Coleman jumped in to try and ease the tension that had enveloped them all by simply asking her sister-in-law,

"Lois, could you please start passing the potatoes around?"

Irene's words were certainly a breach of etiquette; after all, this was Lois' home and table, not Irene's, and taking the lead in who would be served what food, in what order, was immutably reserved for Lois. Lois took no offense, though, and without saying anything, sent a "thank you" message to Irene with her eyes as she reached for the bowl of mashed potatoes and handed them to Irene on her left.

The uneasy silence eventually gave way to idle chatter among those sitting in the Walker's dining room, and in a way Marty's "grace" actually had a beneficial result: no one dared bring up the war during the entire meal. No doubt talk of the Philippines and Wake Island, Singapore and Malaysia, France, Moscow, and Tobruk would have otherwise dominated the conversation. But while those locations and what was happening at each of them was certainly on everyone's minds, for an hour those thoughts were at least kept off of everyone's lips as other topics were discussed. The closest anyone got to the war was the discussion of home defense measures like the imminent rationing and blackout curtains, but the conversation never ventured overseas where mostly horrific and depressing news abounded.

Later, the main course and side dishes having been devoured, Lois Walker rose from her place to start clearing dinner plates in preparation for homemade apple pie and coffee (milk, of course, for the youngest children rather than coffee). Irene Coleman insisted on helping her sister-in-law clear the table, and when the two were alone in the kitchen Lois turned to Irene and quietly said,

"I'm sorry about what Marty said..."

"It's OK," Irene interrupted, "I keep hearing the same thing from Joseph almost every day."

"But not during grace, I'll bet," Lois countered.

Irene allowed herself a small, almost sad smile.

"No," she agreed. "I have no idea why those two are so eager to get into the war. It will find both of them soon enough."

"How about Jonathan?" Lois asked. "I can't imagine him saying anything like 'I can't wait to kill me some Japs.' I guess he's a more sensible boy than my Marty is, perhaps?"

Irene knew the unspoken end of Lois' sentence— "...and also your Joseph?"—but she took no offense, of course, given her own uneasiness with her son's sentiments.

"I'm not sure," Irene replied to the question about Jonathan, "it's not just being sensible or anything like that."

She paused, not sure if she should continue. Irene Coleman made it a habit never to burden anyone with her worries about her own family, but for some reason she found herself welcoming this brief opportunity to unburden herself to her sister-in-law.

"I think he has things on his mind," Irene continued talking about Jonathan. "I'm not sure what, maybe problems with Francine, but also I think he is as worried about this war as Gerald and I are. Joseph is still a boy, Jonathan is almost a man... and I think Jonathan has a man's view of what war means that Joseph and Marty don't."

"Problems with Francine?" Lois asked, locking onto those words. Francine Donner was a twice-removed cousin by marriage to Lois, the same age as Jonathan Coleman, and had been going steady with Jonathan since near the end of their junior year at Schenley High School. After high school Francine had enrolled in one of Pittsburgh's secretarial schools and was close to graduation. Lois saw the young woman only occasionally, the last time about a month earlier around Thanksgiving.

"I'm not sure," Irene replied. "I know that Jonathan didn't go out with her last night, and he was moping around the house and seemed even more depressed than he's been lately."

The sound of Stan Walker's voice getting louder and more excited caught both women's attentions, and they each grabbed one of the pie plates, Lois also grabbing the steaming coffee pot, and headed back from the kitchen into the dining room.

Gerald Coleman had been right earlier that morning. He was sitting quietly, listening to his brother-in-law say how he had heard a rumor at work that Ford Motor Company out in Detroit was going to get a big tank contract soon—the tank treads would be made at a war plant on Pittsburgh's north side, that's how the word got out—and how as soon as he had a few extra bucks together he'd seriously think about buying some Ford Motor stock.

❀ ❀ ❀

Charlene Coleman had a secret. And like most secrets of young women, this one cried out to be conspiratorially shared with a trusted confidant.

During the years the two families lived together in the Coleman house, the children going off in twos or threes to one bedroom or another in the house or out in the yard became a regular after-meal ritual. Jonathan, Marty, and Joseph had been a regular trio, while Charlene and her one-year-younger cousin Lorraine had been just as close. Whereas the trio of the oldest boys had spent most of their time talking about "boys' stuff"—baseball and other sports, mostly—the girls spent most of their time talking about boys in their school, even as far back as their early teens. (The older Coleman and Walker boys eventually began working girls into their conversations as they got older, but rarely deeper than trying to figure out the sexual mysteries they were confronting for the first time.)

Charlene and Lorraine had shared their respective firsts in glorious (and occasionally embellished) detail. That first goodnight kiss on a date; that first time fending off a boy's wandering hands; that first time yielding to a boy's wandering hands...

And now Charlene had "the secret" that she had to share with her cousin.

"I'm engaged!" she blurted out a split second after Lorraine had shut her bedroom door.

Lorraine Walker spun around, open-mouthed and wide-eyed, her eyes automatically looking down at her cousin's ring finger.

Charlene caught her cousin's gaze, and looked down at her own ring finger and then back at Lorraine.

"I don't have a ring, I wouldn't dare!" she giggled.

"Tell me everything!" Lorraine said excitedly, the volume of her own voice dropping as if leading Charlene to do the same.

And so Charlene Coleman did tell her cousin everything. She told how the previous night Larry had picked her up at 7:30 in his father's old Hudson Super Six that Mr. Moncheck still nursed along, somehow keeping it running (most of the time, anyway). They went to see Joan Fontaine in *Suspicion* but Charlene saw even less of the movie than usual since Larry had begun taking her on movie dates, always steering her towards corner seats in the theater's back row. The newsreel had barely begun and Larry had his arm around Charlene, pulling her towards him and kissing her passionately. By the time Joan Fontaine made her first appearance on the screen Larry's fingers were already teasing at one of Charlene's nipples through her Angora sweater. And by the movie's end Charlene's brassiere was unhooked and Larry's right hand was roaming freely over the sensitive skin of her breasts.

They went parking on Mount Washington afterwards, Larry's car pulled up against the railing and overlooking the downtown city lights filtering through the soft, steady snowfall. Charlene couldn't stop shivering from the duality of the cold along with the delicious desire that kept sweeping over her in waves as Larry resumed his handiwork. Larry, bolstered by this turn of events— Charlene had always stopped him by now, never giving him more than five or ten minutes beneath her brassiere— began to shift his attention and efforts to lower regions, but now Charlene halted his advances, clamping her right hand firmly on Larry's left wrist as his fingers toyed with the bottom hem of her skirt, slowly edging higher from her knees along her thighs.

"Don't!" she told him firmly but then softened the rejection by leaning over to kiss Larry, her tongue seeking out his. After a minute Larry tried again, but the result was the same: turned away at the gate, so to speak.

Leaning back in the driver's seat of the Hudson, Larry reached into his jacket pocket and grabbed a pack of Lucky Strikes. Lighting one, he flicked another an inch out of the pack and held it towards Charlene, who took the cigarette and lit it off of Larry's.

"I'm enlisting right after New Year's," he said suddenly.

Charlene looked over at him with alarm, but he kept staring ahead, his eyes refusing to meet hers.

"I turn 18 on January 2nd," he continued, "so I don't need my old man's permission."

He finally turned to look at Charlene.

"I'm thinking of the Marines, but I haven't decided for sure yet. I'm not sure if they'll take me, so maybe the Army instead, I don't know."

Charlene finally spoke.

"Why?"

A slight smirk, or maybe it was a touch of a sad smile, took hold of Larry's lips, and he shrugged his shoulders.

"Why not?" he answered. "I'll get drafted sooner or later—probably sooner than later—I might as well get it over with."

"But what about the rest of school?" Charlene asked.

"I'm not sure," he replied. "They might not take me right away and make me finish school, or maybe they'll ship me right off to basic training that same day. I'm not sure."

He took a deep drag on his cigarette, staring back out the windshield, before continuing.

"But what's the point?" He looked back at Charlene. "I mean, look at everything that's happening... school seems so... I don't know..."

He reached out both of his hands and grasped both of hers.

"If they send me off soon, I want you to wait for me..."

"Of course I will," Charlene interrupted him.

He shook his head.

"No, you don't know what I mean. I want to know that if I'm off fighting the Japs or the Germans that you're back here, waiting for me to come back. And I want to have something to remember you by..."

Charlene had the sudden thought that Larry had shifted his tactics to a version of "I'm going off to war, let me make love to you, just one wonderful time, because I may not come back..."

But the next words out of Larry's mouth surprised Charlene.

"I want us to get engaged before they send me away," he said. As if realizing that a proper proposal should be a question, not a statement, he tried again.

"Charlene, will you marry me? I mean, I know we can't get married right away without your parents' permission, but we can get engaged now and as soon as you turn eighteen I can get back here on leave if I can and we can get married then, it's less than a year and a half away. Or we can..."

As if realizing that his mouth runneth over, he abruptly cut himself off, and repeated his primary question.

"Will you marry me?"

❀ ❀ ❀

Charlene paused in her story.

"And you said yes?" Lorraine asked her.

"Uh-huh," Charlene replied. "But we agreed to keep it a secret, at least for now, until Larry enlists and finds out if he's leaving right away or next spring after school is over. I figure my mother will probably find out soon enough…"

Out of a curious sort of child-to-parent respect, Charlene wouldn't elaborate any further, as if to talk about her mother's inevitable objection to her daughter's engagement three months shy of her seventeenth birthday to a boy Irene didn't particularly care for and who was contemplating dropping out of high school would be in some way disloyal. A mother-daughter battle would ensue soon enough; no point in dwelling on the particulars before they happened.

"Did he give you a ring?" Lorraine asked.

"No," Charlene shook her head, knowing that her cousin's next question would be the same one Charlene had asked herself nearly a dozen times since the previous night.

"Well, are you really engaged if he didn't give you a ring? I mean, he asked you and everything but…"

As if intuitively and instantly sensing that she had struck a raw nerve, Lorraine abruptly stopped speaking, but Charlene picked up that thread, seeking some sort of affirmation from her cousin that this whole engagement wasn't just a charade.

"He told me that he'd get me a ring before he ships out for boot camp, whenever that will be, and I can wear it then. Larry said that if he gave me a ring now I'd have to keep it hidden anyway, and besides my mother might accidentally find it before I had a chance to figure out how to tell her."

Charlene leaned back on her cousin's bed against the wall, wishing that she had a cigarette at this very moment; she certainly could use one.

"I asked Larry the same thing," Charlene continued, "how could we be engaged if he wasn't even giving me an engagement ring? I mean, it doesn't have to be an expensive one, I know he doesn't have a lot of money, but every time I've seen a man ask a woman to marry her in the movies he always gives her a ring..."

"Maybe he'll give you a ring for Christmas as a surprise gift!" Lorraine interrupted excitedly.

Charlene shook her head.

"I already thought of that, but if that was his plan then he would have waited to ask me on Christmas Day when he gave me the ring instead of last night, right?"

A sly look came to Lorraine's face.

"Maybe he just blurted it out because you two were, you know..."

Charlene blushed and chuckled.

"I don't know, maybe. Anyway, as far as I'm concerned I'm engaged, ring or no ring. If he doesn't give me a ring before he ships out then I guess the engagement is off, but that's probably a couple months away at least."

"So what happened next?" Lorraine asked.

Charlene blushed even more, her face now looking as if it were the following spring and she had just instantaneously received her first sunburn of the season. But this time, she didn't answer her cousin's question—verbally, anyway, even though her face gave away part of the answer. She didn't tell Lorraine how Larry had pulled her towards him again and began to kiss her again, and then again moved his left hand under her sweater. She didn't tell Lorraine how, after about a minute stroking her breasts he withdrew his hand and began again to fiddle with the edge of her skirt as he rested the side of his hand against the inside of Charlene's upper right thigh, slowly and almost imperceptibly vibrating his hand back and forth against her bare skin.

Charlene didn't tell Lorraine how this time she didn't stop Larry until about ten minutes later when he maneuvered to slide his fingers inside her panties; newly engaged or not, Charlene finally snapped out of her near-trance to put a stop to Larry's hands for the evening. But Charlene also didn't tell Lorraine how before she finally did stop him, she had allowed Larry's hand under her skirt for the first time, stroking the outside of her underwear and finally touching and rubbing her with only a thin layer of fabric between his fingers and that most sensitive and previously private place on her body.

After all, Charlene thought to herself the previous night and again today in her cousin's bedroom, Larry Moncheck was now her fiancé, and they had simply celebrated their impending union by Charlene permitting Larry a new level of previously off-limits intimacy.

And besides, as of two weeks ago the times had certainly changed... and quite possibly old rules no longer applied.

❀ ❀ ❀

The two sets of parents were still sitting in the dining room, clustered around the oak table, drinking their third and fourth cups of coffee and smoking their Pall Malls and Old Golds. With the children gone the talk had turned to the war; mostly it was Stan Walker and Gerald Coleman who did the talking, but Irene and Lois chimed in occasionally, mostly when the conversation drifted into Home Front matters.

"You wouldn't believe all the troop trains Penn Central is putting together," Stan Walker said, snuffing out the dwindling remnants of an Old Gold after using it to light his next one. "And we have hundreds of boxcars going all over the place that are guarded by soldiers with guns; I guess they're carrying more guns and spare parts and what have you."

Stan paused, appearing to be contemplating something, before continuing.

"I tell you, I hate the reason for it, but this war is the best thing for us economically."

Stan didn't notice—or perhaps was ignoring—the look of disgust that came over Gerald Coleman's face as he continued.

"Things were hopping before because of everything that we were shipping to England and Russia for Lend-Lease, but just in the past week I swear I've never seen so much activity around the clock. I hear that the war plants already can't find enough workers; a couple of years ago, who woulda thought we'd ever see that happen?"

Gerald had an overwhelming urge to shut up his brother-in-law and his "this war is great for business" one-track mind. So he did.

"Speaking of war plants," Gerald said, putting his coffee cup down on the saucer with a hint of authority indicating that something monumentally important was about to be said, "I'm going down tomorrow to that plant you were talking about on the north side that's gonna make tank treads and apply for a job."

The other three adults looked over at him, Irene's face wearing a look of astonishment that told her husband "I can't believe you're saying this without telling me first!"

"What about your shoe repair store? You giving that up?" Stan wanted to know, as surprised as his sister at what Gerald had just said.

"No," Gerald shook his head, "I can keep doing shoe repairs at night when I get home and when I'm off-shift, like on Sundays... if I even get the job, I haven't even applied yet, I don't know that there's any openings left at that place. But if they're filled up I'll try one of the other plants; like Stan says, they all really need workers now."

"I don't understand," Irene finally spoke, leaving behind the why-didn't-you-tell-me-first issue (though Gerald would certainly get an earful when they got back to their own house), "why do you need to take two jobs now? Things are doing OK at the shop, right?"

"It's not that," Gerald Coleman answered his wife. "It's not how much business there is, though I'll tell you, I think business will slow down soon because of all the men and boys who will be leaving for the service. But I figure that if Jonathan and Joseph"—he looked over at Stan and Lois—"and also Marty, and all these other kids are going off to war, then the least I can do is do my part back here rather than just pretend that things are the same as they always have been."

"You could always enlist yourself," Stan Walker said, and immediately both his own wife and his sister each shot him the same incredulous will-you-*please*-shut-up-already! look.

"What?" Stan said defensively, "Gerald is 43 so he can't get drafted, but I was just reading last week about some guy from East Liberty who was 42 or 43, I forget which, he has six or seven kids, anyway this guy went down and enlisted in the Army as a buck private. His picture was in the *Sun-Telegraph* from that enlistment station down on Butler Street, getting sworn in and everything."

He looked over at his brother-in-law.

"You already were in the Army once, you'd be ahead of the game when it came to all these young kids. Hell, maybe they'd even make you an officer."

Out of the corner of his eye Gerald caught the my-God-don't-you-even-think-about-it! glare from his wife.

"I was never much of a soldier anyway," Gerald replied, "I wouldn't be much help in combat to these kids."

A look of resolve was apparent to all as he suddenly sat up straight in his chair.

"But I *will* do my part, just like you're doing, Stan, with your job on the railroads. I have to for my sons and your son and all the others."

What Gerald didn't say—what none of them dared say, or even think—was that Gerald's rationale was more than a simplistic "support the troops" gesture of solidarity. Rather, given the tenor of the first two weeks of this new war for America, and the two-plus years that had come earlier, every little bit of support from ordinary, insignificant people such as Gerald Coleman might very well mean the difference between their collective survival or—God help them all—some radically altered and oppressive new way of living under Hitler or Tojo.

"So what do you think?" Joseph Coleman asked his cousin Marty as they threw around a football in the street in front of the Walker house in the afternoon chill, slopping through the brownish-gray slush that was now all that was left from the previous day's snowfall. Marty would occasionally take a throw from Joseph and wing the ball at his cousin Jonathan, the former Schenley High football star who was standing by the curb, half-participating in the football tossing but mostly staying out of the conversation.

"I don't know," Marty said. "I figure if I join the Marines I'll definitely go to the Pacific, you know, with all those islands and everything, that's what the Marines do."

"I'm thinking about either flying with the Navy or the Air Corps..."

"But don't you need to be an officer to be a pilot?" Marty asked. "And don't you need to be a college graduate to fly?"

"I heard they're changing those rules cause they need pilots so badly," Joseph replied. "I really want to fly..."

"You can fly in the Marines, too," Marty countered. "I figure the Marines are the toughest bunch, that's the place to be to see lots of action."

Catching the football again from Joseph and again flinging it to his cousin Jonathan, Marty asked,

"How about you, Jonny? You decide yet where you're going to join up?"

"Nah," Jonathan shook his head, catching the football from his cousin and instead of sending it on to his brother, he whipped it back to Marty with extra zip this time, guaranteed to cause a sting in his cousin's hands when the high-velocity pass arrived in the cold... a sting that hopefully conveyed the message that Jonathan had no interest in jabbering about the Army or Navy or Marines or Air Corps, or anything to do with the war.

"Ow!" Marty yelped involuntarily as his cousin's pass smacked into his hands and then bounced to the cobblestone street, sending up a spray of the dirty slush onto his khakis. He went to retrieve the football and tossed it this time to Joseph.

Jonathan Coleman felt a twinge of regret at having zipped the ball with such force at his cousin, but he was still irritated at Marty—and his brother—as they two resumed their musings about which military service they would join, how they couldn't want to "see action" (vernacular they both picked up from the war movies, obviously), and different scenarios in which each could be a hero and get his picture on the cover of *Life*, smiling and bedecked with medals and service ribbons.

Kids, Jonathan thought, even though he was only two years older than both his brother and cousin; but two years was a world of difference, especially at their respective ages. At seventeen, still months away from being exposed to the military draft, Marty and Joseph could well afford to treat their inevitable military service in much the same way that they had played soldier in the Coleman house's front yard in their younger years... little more than a fantasy, a game in which they could fashion the outcome. And even if they "lost," big deal; it was all just a game.

But Jonathan Coleman realized that what faced them all was nothing even close to a game; it was so very, very real. And it wasn't so much combat with the enemy that Jonathan feared (though he certainly had no desire to experience actual war any sooner than necessary), but rather the indecision and confusion that sometimes bordered on panic among "people in charge."

Take the latest Home Front defenses that had been frantically concocted over the past two weeks, Jonathan thought. On the one hand, all homes must have blackout curtains in place by nightfall, so no residential city lights would be visible from the air. But many of the downtown stores seemed oblivious to these restrictions, apparently more interested in attracting Christmas shoppers than adhering to wartime mandates. And speaking of Christmas shoppers, at night a steady stream of automobiles and streetcars trudged up and down the major thoroughfares into and out of downtown; even with the mandatory shielding above the cars' headlights, enough collective light reflected off of the wet streets and seeped upwards for any overhead enemy bombers to detect and thus determine that they were above a major population center.

And how about the searchlights that had been installed around most of the major steel plants on the outskirts of the city and in up-river towns such as New

Kensington and Kittanning? Sure, the residential areas were blacked out, but the big steel plants seemed to have their own rules and had their surrounding searchlights lighting up the skies periodically throughout the night, seeking out any invading German bombers that perhaps had sneaked up on the East Coast much as the Japanese fleet had done two weeks earlier in Hawaii. Or maybe they were conducting exercises, test runs for their new gunnery crews. Either way, how much sense did it make to have high-intensity searchlights beaming up from every high-profile war target in or near the city, sweeping the skies for enemy bombers all night, rather than keep the searchlights shut down and turning them on only if a German bomber fleet were positively spotted closer to the eastern seaboard and headed west, long before arriving anywhere near Pittsburgh?

So many inconsistencies, Jonathan thought, and the same people making these puzzling and often conflicting decisions—or other people just like them—would be the ones who would be making policy decisions that would dictate where Jonathan Coleman might possibly face the forces of one of the country's enemies. Given how the war had been going so far, the odds would likely be against Jonathan's side when the engagement came, but unlike a Schenley High football game against one of the city's stronger teams during the years that Jonathan played and starred, a game plan to help overcome the American side's underdog status seemed to be nowhere in sight. And, of course, the consequences of losing a battle or the war itself were far, far more disastrous than those of losing a City League high school football game to Peabody or Westinghouse.

Jonathan looked over at his brother and his cousin in time to see the football coming in his direction again, this time from Joseph. He caught the ball easily, and then flicked it to Marty with far less velocity than the previous time. After all, the two of them were really just kids, Jonathan thought; they'd grow up soon enough and who knew, one or both of them might be killed or seriously wounded in the war in the not-too-distant future. Might as well let them be kids and live in their fantasy world a little bit longer, Jonathan thought.

Besides, Jonathan had other worries on his mind than the war. As Irene Coleman had told Lois Walker earlier in the kitchen, something might very well be askew in Jonathan's relationship with Francine Donner. Saturday nights were *always* spent together, boyfriend-girlfriend, especially after two years together... as was true of Jonathan and Francine. Family occasions, parentally mandated trips to see out-of-town grandparents, and emergencies were acceptable exceptions, of course; Francine going out with Donnie Yablonski because he was shipping off to Navy boot camp the day after Christmas, no matter which way Jonathan looked at it, was not.

Like Jonathan, Donnie had been a two-sport athlete at Schenley, both football and baseball. While Jonathan was the star of the football team and also a pretty decent baseball player, Donnie was the opposite: good enough on the football field to start at halfback on offense and also as defensive back though not as good as Jonathan, who was a second team all-city selection. Donnie, though, was an outstanding baseball player, skilled enough to get a tryout with the Pirates right out of high school. The Pirates didn't sign him, but the head scout running the tryout session told Donnie to come back in a year or two after he picked up more experience.

More relevant to Jonathan's predicament, Donnie Yablonski had gone steady with Francine for the two years before she broke up with him to begin dating Jonathan. There had been a bit of tension between Jonathan and Donnie for a few weeks in the aftermath of that switch, but after Donnie began dating Carol Lawrence all was forgotten.

But when Donnie Yablonski called Francine the previous Monday to tell her that he had enlisted in the Navy and was assigned the last slot at Boot Camp starting right after Christmas, and when he asked Francine if she would go out with him one last time Saturday night "just for old time's sake," Francine couldn't say no to an "old friend" going off to war. At least that's how Francine put it when she called Jonathan on Tuesday to tell him that they wouldn't be going out this coming Saturday. After recovering from the shock of hearing his girlfriend tell him that she planned on going out with her old boyfriend instead of him, Jonathan proposed a Friday night date instead of Saturday, but Francine declined, saying that her entire family was having dinner at her grandmother's that evening.

"It's only for one night," Francine tried to soothe Jonathan on the phone, "he'll be gone soon enough afterwards. I just couldn't say no to him, he started talking about all the old times we had had together..."

Francine's words blurred to a hum as Jonathan's mind whirled. I'll kill that sneaky son of a bitch before the Japs ever get a hand on him, Jonathan thought. His first impulse was to go around the corner to Donnie's house, grab him by his shirt, and demand to know just what in the world he thought he was doing.

But Donnie was his friend (or so Jonathan thought, but now he wasn't quite so certain) and besides, he knew that Francine wouldn't take very kindly to her boyfriend acting like a jealous kid. So Jonathan just gritted his teeth, told Francine that he would see her the following week before Christmas to give her her present, and he did everything he could to steer clear of running into Donnie over the next few days so the subject of his friend's apparent betrayal didn't have to be discussed at all.

For the next few days, Jonathan was fairly successful in keeping both Donnie and Francine from his mind, exhausted as he was from his prolonged workday. But when Saturday night finally arrived, the full force of what was happening hit him, and no matter what he did he couldn't get out of his mind that at that very moment his girlfriend was on a date with Donnie Yablonski. Donnie could be kissing her at that very moment, or maybe doing even more!

Occasionally the logical portion of his mind would take control of his thoughts, and he'd remember that Donnie and Francine had gone steady when they were in tenth and eleventh grades, and that right after Francine had broken up with Donnie (but before he knew that she had her eye on Jonathan) Donnie had told Jonathan that she didn't put out at all beyond kissing in the front seat of his car or in the movies. She wouldn't even get into the back seat of Donnie's Packard, words Jonathan assumed at the time were intended to tell Jonathan that "winning" Francine from him would be a hollow victory.

But Jonathan and Francine had been going steady at more advanced and mature points in their respective young lives, and she had shown no such reluctance after the first few months with Jonathan. He still hadn't gone all the way with her, but their necking sessions were of such intensity and "up to the limits" that Jonathan figured it was only a matter of time.

Besides, he planned on asking Francine to marry him, and he planned on doing so very soon... in fact, later this very week when he gave her her Christmas present, the engagement ring he planned to buy tomorrow when shopping downtown with his parents, brothers, and sisters... the engagement ring that would clean out a significant chunk of the money he had been saving since he had started working full-time right after high school graduation. He had decided right after Thanksgiving to ask Francine to marry him, and had planned on waiting until Christmas to do so. After the attack on Pearl Harbor two weeks earlier Jonathan had felt an overwhelming impulse and sense of urgency to buy a ring and ask Francine the following day or the day after that, but he decided not to do it that way, thinking it would seem as if he were simply reacting to the outbreak of war.

No, he'd stay the course, he had decided. But now on Sunday afternoon, as he contemplated the aftermath of Francine and Donnie together the night before, he worried that maybe he hadn't made the right decision; that if he had asked Francine ten or twelve days earlier (and if she had said yes, which he was confident that she would), there was no way she would have gone out with Donnie last night.

Well, Jonathan thought, what's done is done; no sense in worrying about it now. He turned his head when he heard his mother call to Joseph and him that it was time for them all to go home, and he caught one last pass from Marty after hearing his cousin yell "Jonny! Heads up!" Jonathan cradled the football thoughtfully, his thoughts still lost between two subjects he wished he could get out of his mind: the war, and Francine agreeing to go out on a date with Donnie Yablonski.

2—Monday, December 22, 1941

The morning *Post-Gazette* brought a bit of good news from the two war fronts.

Brits Sink 4 U-Boats

Germans Attack Convoy; Brits Lose Only One Ship

And also, in the right-most column, some potentially encouraging (but still tenuous) news from the Pacific:

Relief on Way to Wake Island

U.S. Navy Approaches, But Japs Still Bombing

Gerald Coleman quickly skimmed the two stories and the others on the front page, and felt a bit heartened that on both fronts crushing defeat for America and Britain hopefully wasn't imminent. Still, his resolve to get a job at the north side war plant hadn't weakened overnight. Quite possibly, these two small bits of good news were being emphasized by the newspapers over whatever other horrors were occurring on other Pacific islands or elsewhere in Europe or the North Atlantic; Gerald had no idea, nor did he think any other average guy like him did either.

Gerald was never one for lingering leisurely at the breakfast table after finishing his bacon and eggs, but this morning it seemed to Irene Coleman that her husband was much more anxious than usual. For the first time in his adult life, he would be walking into an office and asking someone to give him a job, rather than have his fate in his own hands as his own boss. Even during the Great Depression he had been able to maintain his independence, answering to no one but himself and his customers. But as he insisted to Irene the previous evening after they returned home from the Walkers' house, if his sons would soon be unfailingly taking direction from others—boot camp drill sergeants at first and then squad leaders and company commanders in the midst of combat—then for at least the next few years, then Gerald Coleman could do the same in far less of a life-and-death situation than his sons would be facing.

He bundled up in his overcoat, put on his galoshes at Irene's insistence, and plopped his hat on his head before trudging out the door just as the clock was striking 7:30 A.M. Then he stopped at the doorway and turned back to Irene, who was standing slightly behind him, wiping her hands on her apron as she prepared to shut the front door behind her husband. Gerald leaned over, a bit off balance, and kissed Irene goodbye... something he almost never did when he left for the shoe shop in the morning. Gerald Coleman certainly loved his wife, but he was typically never one for demonstrating his affection with kisses or touches during the day, preferring instead to wait for the occasional nights when they would quickly and quietly make love before giving in to their exhaustion to grab a few hours of sleep.

But today seemed to mark a kind of new beginning, at least in Gerald Coleman's work life, and for some reason he thought that a kiss was appropriate for the situation. Irene, caught a bit off guard but not complaining (she often wished her husband was more demonstrative with his affection, but she accepted the way he was), kissed him back, and also reached up to gently place her left hand against his right cheek, a gesture of empathetic affection that needed no accompanying words.

She shut the door behind him, noting that the morning's flurries had already stopped, but the day seemed as if it would be even colder than yesterday or the day before. No surprise, winter was now officially one day old, though Irene Coleman knew with certainty that this year's winter, the darkest and deepest winter they would ever know, had actually started fifteen days earlier around noontime on December 7th.

Irene turned her attention back to fixing breakfast for the children, who would soon be trickling one by one into the kitchen. Today marked the beginning of a short break from school for the youngest four, a break that would last until the day after New Year's. In years past the school break had been even shorter, beginning on Christmas Eve or the last school day before December 24th if Christmas Eve fell on a weekend. But this year, the city's school officials decided that a slightly longer break was in order, partly to give children a bit more time at home with their families amidst the new war turmoil, but mostly to save on the heating and lighting of the school buildings during a few extra frigid Pittsburgh December days.

Sleeping in a bit later than usual was a luxury Irene granted her children during their break from school, though she had no intention of having her children lull around in bed until late in the morning. If anyone was still in bed past 7:45 she would wake them, but she knew that especially today, with Christmas shopping coming later that day, none of the children would need to be rousted from their respective beds.

The first child to arrive in the kitchen was six-year old Ruth. No surprise, Irene thought; if possible, Ruth would drag her mother downtown for Christmas shopping immediately after breakfast, even though the stores weren't open yet. To a girl Ruth's age, the delay of more than a week in the Colemans' annual downturn sojourn might as well have been an eternity, and every day Ruth pouted when her mother told her that no, they couldn't go downtown today, the trip would have to wait for just a bit longer.

Preempting the question she knew was coming from her daughter, Irene kissed the girl on her forehead and asked,

"You know what we're going to do tonight, don't you?"

"Go downtown to see Santa and look for Crispmas presents?" Ruth still pronounced Christmas as "Crispmas," much to the amusement of her brothers and sister—especially Thomas, who still teased his younger sister about her pronunciation—but Irene figured that soon enough, the girl would get the word right.

"Uh-huh," Irene nodded, prompting a big grin on Ruth's face and an excited burst of hand clapping.

Just then Thomas walked into the kitchen and turning to Ruth, asked,

"Hey Ruthie, today we're going 'Crispmas' shopping, right?"

"Leave her alone, Thomas," Irene Coleman chided her son, but given the good nature of his teasing, she didn't say anything else. The truth be told, a bit of sibling bickering was always a welcome part of the Coleman home. When Jonathan and Joseph had been younger—actually, even up to a few years earlier—the two had relentlessly picked on one another, Joseph instigating more than his share despite being two years younger than his brother. Then it had been Joseph and Charlene, and later Charlene and Thomas, until about two years ago when Charlene had entered high school and abruptly adopted an attitude of "I can't waste my time with a little kid" towards her younger brother. To Irene, though, the nonstop, mostly harmless bickering through the years brought life into her home, and she welcomed it.

One by one, the other children, all except Jonathan who was at work, wandered into the kitchen. (Irene still thought of them all, even Jonathan, as children.) Joseph, the last to arrive, picked up the *Post-Gazette* and noting the headlines, grinned and held the paper towards Thomas.

"See, what did I tell you? We're already sinking U-boats and the Japs won't know what hit them when the Marines get into it."

Irene sighed and looked over at Joseph with that particular look that unfailingly told its recipient that he or she had done or said something that displeased her.

"Don't start, Joseph," she warned. "Just for one day, let's not talk about the war, OK?"

Though Irene had seemingly asked her son a question, Joseph Coleman knew that his mother had actually issued a command worthy of any he would someday hear from a Marine drill sergeant, and as with the drill sergeant, his mother *would* be obeyed. He simply nodded, and reached for the serving plate filled with scrambled eggs to help himself.

The children began to chatter among themselves, telling each other what they most wanted for Christmas. Despite moving through a blur of kitchen duties—refilling milk glasses, putting second helpings onto plates, cooking more food as needed—Irene's mind meticulously recorded this latest list of each child's and simultaneously kept running tallies of her best guesses of the costs of those gifts, like a human tabulating machine. Some of the lowest-priced items would be purchased as gifts from one child to another, helping to bring each child closer to a merry Christmas—gift-wise, at least—this year.

"So what is your boyfriend going to give you?" Joseph suddenly asked Charlene in a voice that was half-teasing, as if the two of them were several years younger and Joseph was taunting his sister with a cry of "Charlene's got a boyfriend; Charlene's got a boyfriend" as he had when he had found out about the first boy who was interested in his sister.

Irene turned around just in time to see Charlene flinch slightly before she muttered "I don't know" and lowered her eyes to her plate. Irene instantly knew that something was up, but she didn't pursue the matter; she'd find out soon enough, she always did.

As each child finished breakfast, Irene cleared the dirty plates from the table and gave each a light rinse under the faucet, stacking the dishes on one side of the double sink until they were all ready to be washed before she headed out for her morning errands. Seemingly at a loss for what to do this morning—no school, no regularly scheduled Saturday morning chores, no Sunday morning church—the four of them lounged around the living room. Joseph flicked on the radio to the voice of Arthur Godfrey, but he rolled the dial searching for NBC Radio and the tail end of *National Farm and Home Hour*, knowing that the next program— *News of Europe*—would be starting in minutes.

Thomas grabbed the *Post-Gazette's* sports section—without Pirates baseball and the college football season all but over the sports section was rather light, but the city's minor league hockey team, the Pittsburgh Hornets, had played the night before and Joseph could read about the hockey game as well as any news of the upcoming football bowl games on New Year's Day. For more than a week there had been rumors circulating that the bowl games would be canceled because of the war, but for now anyway, the games were still scheduled.

Ruth went up to her room to get one of her coloring books and some of her crayon stubs to bring back to the living room. Maybe Santa will bring me some new crayons for Crispmas, she thought, and vowed that she'd remember to ask Santa tonight in Gimbel's.

And, as Irene peeked into the living room to look in on her children, she saw Charlene sitting on the sofa, staring at the wall across the room, a contemplative look on her face.

I'll find out soon enough, Irene told herself again, and went back into the kitchen to make short work of the dishes.

Two streetcar transfers later, Gerald Coleman exited the red and white car only a block and a half from the front entrance of what had long ago been an automobile manufacturing plant, back in the early days of motorcars when hundreds, if not thousands, of manufacturers and brands could be found in all corners of the country. Gerald couldn't recall the name of this particular auto manufacturer since it had gone out of business even before the Great Depression took almost all of them under, leaving only a handful of manufacturers left, most of them clustered in or near Detroit. For almost a decade and a half this red brick building with its oversized windows, each window comprised of hundreds of panes of opaque glass— and most of those panes eventually broken over the years— had stood vacant. Now, Gerald could see the workmen frantically putting in new glass panes to replace the broken ones, as well as a steady stream of people walking into and out of—mostly into—the building's entranceway.

For a moment a feeling of panic swept over Gerald. Maybe I'm too late and all the jobs are taken, he thought. Well, he figured, if that's the case there are other war plants around now and most likely even more to come, I'm sure I'll find a job somewhere.

He needn't have feared. After waiting only about ten minutes in the reception area where he began filling out the job application he had been handed, he was ushered into the assistant personnel manager's office, who informed him that jobs were so plentiful at the plant, the company's management worried that they wouldn't be able to find enough people to get the manufacturing lines started as quickly as the management—and the Army— wanted.

At the request of the assistant personnel manager— John Grassi was his name, according to the nameplate on the desk across from the seat Gerald occupied—Gerald quickly scribbled the additional information on the application that he hadn't yet filled out, and then handed the completed application to Grassi. Gerald sat quietly in his chair as Grassi skimmed through the information that Gerald had provided.

"So you've never worked anywhere except your shoe shop?" Grassi asked the expected question.

"No sir," Gerald answered, wondering if this would be cause for his application to be rejected.

"No problem," Grassi shrugged, "I'm just surprised you were able to keep your store going during the Depression."

A thought appeared to suddenly come to Grassi, who looked up from the application at Gerald.

"We certainly have a job here for you if you want it," he said, "But you might want to think about something. Up on Mount Washington there is a plant that's just getting started up to make Army shoes and boots, they got a big contract last week from Washington. I was figuring that with your background, you might like it better there, you know, it will be more like what you've been doing."

Before Gerald could reply, John Grassi continued.

"Tell you what," he said. "You go up there and if you get a job and you want to take it, no problem. But if they don't offer you nothin' or if you decide that you don't want to work there, come on back here and we'll have something for you. Sound good to you?"

Gerald couldn't argue with such a deal, and he simply said, "Yes sir, sounds good to me."

"The guy you want to talk to is named Danny Harnchevik, he's the assistant personnel manager there. He's a Polish guy like you…"

Grassi interrupted himself.

"You're Polish, right?"

Gerald nodded, as did Grassi in response. He knew the name "Harnchevik" even if he didn't know the person. No doubt Danny Harnchevik was a brother or cousin of Clyde Harnchevik, who ran the one shoe shop that competed with Gerald for the neighborhood shoe repair business. But Gerald didn't offer this information.

"I figured from your address, you know, up in Polish Hill," referring to the Pittsburgh neighborhood that had at one time been entirely populated by Polish immigrants and still was predominantly Polish.

"My father's original name was Colmnoski," Gerald offered as an explanation, "but the immigration people at Ellis Island changed it to Coleman when he came over."

"Yeah," Grassi nodded, "at least they could pronounce my old man's name so they left it alone, but I know lots of Italians who also had their names changed by the immigration people."

John Grassi rose from his chair, as did Gerald.

"I'll keep this with me," he indicated Gerald's application he was holding in his left hand as he extended his right hand, "just let me know how it goes over there."

Gerald likewise extended his right hand to shake the other man's.

"Thank you very much, sir," Gerald replied and then turned to leave, his mind already calculating which streetcar connections he'd have to make to get over to Mount Washington from the north side, and then figuring that maybe he'd just walk the three or so miles, despite the cold, so he could think this whole double-job situation out.

His thoughts were interrupted by John Grassi who asked, as Gerald was heading out the door, "So you have Army-age sons too, I take it?"

Gerald turned back to face Grassi.

"One who's nineteen right now, another who's seventeen."

He paused for a moment and, as if it were bad luck to leave out a reference to Thomas, he added,

"And another one who's fourteen, if this thing lasts long enough."

"I got one who's twenty and another who's eighteen," Grassi replied, his eyes distant, "plus three more trailing behind them."

He paused before continuing.

"I hope your boys stay safe," he said.

"Yours too," Gerald replied.

"Hello?"

Mrs. Donner again, not Francine.

"Hello, Mrs. Donner, this is Jonathan Coleman again. I was wondering if Francine was there?"

The same hesitancy as the last time Jonathan had called an hour and a half earlier from the pay phone up on Smallman Street, a short block from the *J. Weisberg & Sons* produce wholesaler where he worked.

"I'm sorry, Jonathan, she's still not home." Mrs. Donner's voice was flat, measured, as if she was speaking words she had previously rehearsed and was carefully trying not to reveal... something.

"Do you expect her back soon?" Jonathan asked the same question he had asked three hours earlier. This time, Mrs. Donner's tone conveyed a touch of agitation.

"I told you that I'm not certain where she is or when she'll be home," came the irritated reply.

Jonathan knew that Mrs. Donner was lying. Francine frequently complained to him about her mother's intrusiveness, demanding everything but a mimeographed schedule every time Francine left the house, day or night. One of the reasons that Francine's mother was fond of Jonathan (or at least as fond as the mother of a nineteen-year old young woman could be towards the young man who was by now no doubt introducing her daughter, little by little, to intimacies that Mrs. Donner still felt should be delayed until marriage) was that Jonathan readily submitted to the mother's grilling questions every time he set foot in the Donner house to collect Francine for a date, and so far had never been caught fibbing about where he planned to take her daughter.

So Jonathan immediately recognized the cool and evasive tone of Mrs. Donner's voice as an indication that things were certainly not as they should be. Francine could very well be at home this very minute and may have also been at home when Jonathan had called the first time, frantically waving her hands at her mother or putting her index finger to her lips, signaling that she didn't want to talk to Jonathan. Or maybe Francine really wasn't at home—maybe she was Christmas shopping downtown, Jonathan had a sudden thought—but if that were the case, that still didn't explain why Mrs. Donner was suddenly treating Jonathan as she never had before.

"Well, could you please tell her I called and that I'm home from work now?" Jonathan hesitated for a minute about what he should say next. If he told Mrs. Donner, as he had done the first time he had called that he'd call back soon, he risked aggravating her even more... not to mention Francine. Or he could tell Mrs. Donner to ask Francine to call him at home, but like most young women, Francine rarely if ever called a young man at home, even her steady boyfriend of nearly two years.

Jonathan decided on the first option; the hell with Mrs. Donner, *he* wasn't the one on this phone conversation lying to the other.

"I'll call back a little bit later then, if you could please tell her when she comes in," he said in a tone as pleasant as he could muster to reply to someone whom he suddenly, intensely disliked.

"Fine," was Mrs. Donner's one-syllable reply and then Jonathan heard the click on the other end as she hung up. He fought the impulse to slam the heavy black metal handset down onto the phone, which would cause the phone's bell to clang as loudly (if only for a second) as if a phone call was coming into the Coleman house. No use taking out his frustration on the phone, and besides one the younger Coleman children—probably Ruthie or maybe even Thomas, both of whom were sitting in the living room listening to the radio—would probably fink on him to their mother, just because that's what pesty little brothers and sisters did. Besides, Jonathan was even stronger these days than during his high school football days, courtesy of lugging hundreds of boxes weighing anywhere between fifty and eighty pounds around the *J. Weisberg & Sons* warehouse every day. Ma Bell's phones were sturdy, but all Jonathan needed to do was crack the handset or the phone's casing and there would be hell to pay from both of his parents.

One more time, he told himself, once more later that afternoon, probably around 5:00, he'd call the Donner house again. If he was worrying needlessly in the aftermath of Francine's Saturday night date with Donnie Yablonski, then when he finally got to speak with Francine all his fears would suddenly vanish. But if he still couldn't connect with her, well...

Well what, Jonathan asked himself. What would he do then? Go over to her house? Go to Donnie Yablonski's house? Forget it, the calmer side of Jonathan's mind told him, just stick with the plan and everything will be fine. And the next step of that plan was tonight, when Jonathan would plunk down almost $150 of his hard-earned savings to buy the best diamond engagement ring he could afford for Francine and give it to her when, on Christmas Eve, he would ask her to marry him.

As he did dozens of times most days, Gerald fished into his left trouser pocket for the 1891 Morgan silver dollar that he always carried. The coin's magic or luck or whatever anyone wanted to call it had never failed him before, and it didn't today, either. After meeting with Danny Harnchevik, Gerald was not only the proud new owner of a war plant job, but a job as a day shift supervisor, and at a dollar and a half an hour more than he would have made over on the north side. No doubt Danny Harnchevik figured that if Gerald would be scaling back on his own business to work full-time at the plant each day that his cousin Clyde might pick up some of the piecework from the neighborhood's residents, even some of those who had long used Gerald's services rather than Clyde's.

No matter, Gerald thought as his left thumb ran along the now-smooth edge of the silver dollar as if he were fingering a good-luck charm obtainable from one of the carnival machines at Kennywood Park for a mere penny. The coin's perimeter had been worn smooth by the time his father had handed his son the coin for good on a chilly October morning in 1917 just as Gerald was boarding the train that would take him to the shipyard where he would sail to Europe with thousands of other young American men to join what was now The Great War.

Jo'zef Colmnoski of Krakow had somehow come into possession of this particular American silver dollar coin nearly four years before finally boarding the ship that would take him to the island just off of New York City where he would be renamed John Coleman and begin his journey to become an American. Why "John" and not "Joseph" nobody in the Coleman family—including Jo'zef himself, once he began to learn the English language and its names—could ever understand, save for the possibility that the Ellis Island immigration agent who processed his paperwork was in a particularly bad mood or succumbed to an irrational anger at Jo'zef Colmnoski that afternoon and, vested with the few feeble powers of his job decided that by God, he would rename this foreigner in a way that would let all the Polacks know what their place in their new country would be.

Gerald had heard at least four stories describing how his father had come to possess the coin, none of which was consistent with any of the others. Gerald had never learned which of the stories—or perhaps some other, untold one— was the true story, but he did know that Jo'zef Colmnoski never let that coin get more than a fraction of an inch away from his body during the rest of his days in his native Poland, nor did he change his habits upon his arrival in America.

To Gerald's father, that 1891 silver dollar emitted some form of "positive energy" worthy of any gypsy's talisman. He was convinced that as long as that coin was in his possession, no harm would befall him, and he carried that dollar during the year he spent in Brooklyn apprenticing to a cobbler to learn the trade with which he would get by in this country. He carried that dollar with him when he headed west, first to Altoona for several months at the invitation of a distant cousin and then a bit further west to Pittsburgh, where he settled and opened up his own cobbler shop in 1897, the year his betrothed Natasha finally arrived from the homeland for their long-delayed wedding and a year before their oldest son Gerald was born.

Gerald, in turn, carried his father's gift with him throughout his year and a half on the European continent, and more than once felt that the coin had somehow kept him out of combat and, as wars go, relatively safe. Upon his return to Pittsburgh in early 1919 he offered the coin back to his father who declined, telling Gerald to keep it with him for more good luck when he took over John Coleman's cobbler shop for good, as Gerald did in 1921 just before he married his 20-year old bride.

John Coleman died barely a year later, only weeks after Jonathan was born, and Gerald toyed with the idea of placing the Morgan dollar in his father's coffin, but decided against doing so. His father had never told him explicitly, but Gerald was certain that he would have wanted that coin to continue doing its magic or whatever it was for his descendants, including his brand-new grandson. And so John Coleman—Jo'zef Colmnoski—went to his grave with a little bit of him left behind on the earth above in the form of that 1891 Morgan.

Gerald withdrew his left hand from his pants pocket, leaving the coin behind, to look at his wristwatch. Almost 3:30, the hands on the watch's face told him, and depending on the streetcar connections he'd probably be back at his shop by 4:15, maybe even as early as 4:05 if he got lucky on the connections and the conductor didn't have to slow down too much for traffic congestion.

Still, as anxious as he was to get to the shop and get at least a few heels and soles onto some of the shoes waiting there, he took a short walk past the streetcar stop to Grandview Avenue, the street closest to the edge of the hill that overlooked the Monongahela River below and much of the city beyond. Gerald didn't have much occasion to come to this place for any reason, scenery-gazing or otherwise (his daughter Charlene had been parked with Larry Moncheck in the boy's Hudson Super Six the previous Saturday night only a few feet from where Gerald now stood, but of course he had no way of knowing this), but whenever he did find himself staring down at the city from Mount Washington he always felt that what was happening throughout the city below somehow emanated upward as a single image to its viewer above.

Gerald saw the city alive with the energy of the weeks-old war that was affecting every person's life so deeply. People hustled up and down the downtown streets to offices and stores, the entire panorama beneath him an endless stream of motion and purpose. On the streets closest to the river's opposite edge Gerald could make out people walking with shopping bags no doubt filled with Christmas presents, which reminded Gerald that time was of the essence because of the long-delayed family Christmas shopping trip tonight that would take them to these very streets below.

As he turned away from the view below to head back to the streetcar stop, Gerald's eyes slid upward to the cloud-filled skies above. He then turned back towards the city below but kept his eyes skyward. All the way east, and all the way west, as far as the eye could see in any direction... darkening winter storm clouds that threatened snowfall and intimated other dangers seemed to go on forever.

A chill went through Gerald as he again turned away from the hill's edge and began walking. He reached the streetcar stop just as the red and white electric carriage arrived, and he hopped aboard, mentally calculating the time that would elapse until he hit the transfer station at Liberty Avenue and Smithfield Street near the edge of downtown. Just enough time to grab a newspaper before jumping on the next streetcar for the final part of the trip, Gerald figured.

Ten minutes later, the streetcar having wound its way down from Mount Washington and across the river and through the downtown congestion, Gerald jumped off at the stop and hurried over to the corner newsman, who handed Gerald a hot-off-the-presses afternoon *Pittsburgh Sun-Telegraph* and took Gerald's nickel in return in a smooth, almost poetic motion.

Even though the morning *Post-Gazette* was resting on the Coleman house's front porch every morning, Gerald usually tried to pick up an afternoon *Sun-Telegraph* as well to get the latest news of what happened during the day. Even in his shop Gerald didn't have time to listen to the radio news, busy as he usually was trying to finish the day's work in time to head home for dinner at a reasonable hour. On most days he would grab a *Sun-Telegraph* from the corner market where Irene usually shopped that was halfway between the Coleman house and Gerald's shop, though some days all the store's copies of the afternoon paper would be gone by the time Gerald hit the doors.

Today, though, he could skim the paper while on the next streetcar, even if he couldn't get a seat and had to stand hanging onto one of the car's leather straps. But as soon as he flipped the paper over to look at the headlines, he was sorry that he had yielded to his impulse.

Japs Land on Luzon

Jap Radio Reports Philippine Attack; Imperial Army Heads to Manila

All Gerald could do was slowly shake his head in despair as he began reading.

❀ ❀ ❀

Jonathan Coleman's right index finger hesitated as it rested inside the metallic circle that surrounded the number "7" on the telephone. He began to withdraw his finger and with his left hand return the handset to the phone, but finally decided that he *had* to call Francine back. Suppose she had come home from wherever she had been and was now waiting by the phone for his call? In his heart—and in his gut—Jonathan knew that wasn't the case, but he had told Mrs. Donner that he'd call back, and call back he would.

He knew the number by heart, having dialed it so many times over the past two years, but for a fleeting second Jonathan couldn't remember it; his mind had gone blank and beyond the STerling exchange—the "7" and "8" that were the first two digits—he couldn't remember *any* of the numbers. He felt beads of sweat suddenly appear on his forehead and his neck, and instinctively looked over to the living room radiator that sat along the wall between the room's picture window and the front door. Jonathan knew, however, that a too-high room temperature wasn't the reason for the sudden burst of warmth that had enveloped him; his mother rarely let the temperature in any room in the house get above 65 degrees in any winter, and given the uncertainty about whether or not heating oil would be available this winter and if it was, how much it would cost, Irene Coleman was now keeping the house barely above 60 degrees, even at night.

Nervousness; no other answer for the beads of sweat that were now sliding down Jonathan's forehead onto his eyebrows as well as from his neck down onto his shoulders. Despite the nervousness and the perspiration, the rest of

Francine Donner's phone number popped back into Jonathan's head and he dialed: STerling 1-1037.

Two rings, then three, then four, and just as Jonathan wondered if he should hang up the ringing stopped and a voice answered: Mr. Donner this time instead of his wife.

"Hello?" Unlike Mrs. Donner, Francine's father had always been curt, almost unpleasant, whenever Jonathan had called on Francine. Jonathan could never be certain of the reason. Perhaps he had preferred Donnie Yablonski as a boyfriend for "his little girl," or maybe he imagined Jonathan doing who-knows-what with his daughter simply because Jonathan was the one whom she happened to be dating as she entered womanhood.

Or quite possibly Jack Donner was just a miserable person, angry at the world because he had come so close to losing everything during the Depression, unlike Jonathan's father. Whatever the reason, Jack Donner never seemed glad for the opportunity to engage in any conversation, no matter how short, with Jonathan... and apparently this wouldn't be an exception to that rule.

"Hello, Mr. Donner," Jonathan replied, trying to make his voice sound as pleasant as possible. "Is Francine there?"

No hesitation from Mr. Donner as with his wife.

"She ain't here," he answered gruffly.

Jonathan took in a deep breath through his nose.

"OK, thanks very much. Could you please tell her I called and that I'll try to call her tomorrow, tonight I'm going downtown with..."

"Yeah, all right," Mr. Donner interrupted Jonathan and hung up.

Jonathan held the handset up to his left ear for another second or two, as if the connection would magically rematerialize, this time with Francine on the other end who would provide some type of reasonable explanation for the lack of contact and her parents' unpleasantness.

Maybe I'm too late, Jonathan thought, and for the first time doubt began to creep into his mind and he wondered whether or not he should go ahead and buy her engagement ring as he had planned for months.

Dinner at the Coleman house was a rushed affair this Monday evening, despite Irene Coleman demanding that each of her children "slow down and chew your food!" or else "you'll get an upset stomach and won't be able to go Christmas shopping tonight!"

Her warnings went unheeded, and the dinner that had started at an extra-early 5:30 to leave as much shopping time as possible until the stores closed at 9:30 was all but finished by 5:45. Irene packed the dishes into the sink, mindful of the glares of her children—Thomas and Ruthie in particular—who tried to speed up their mother's cleanup routine through mind over matter. In deference to them and to the evening's special occasion, she resisted her impulse to wash the dishes immediately as she always did after a meal, instead settling for a quick rinse of each plate and then returning each dish to the sink's basin for a more thorough cleaning late that night.

At 6:00, Gerald Coleman led his bundled-up family out the front door and down the street to the streetcar stop, hopefully in time to catch the car that should be by in another five minutes or so if it weren't running ahead of schedule. The thought suddenly occurred to Gerald that so far today he had taken more streetcar rides than previously throughout all of 1941 to date, and yet here were still two more this same day, one more headed downtown and then another back home after the evening's strolling and shopping was concluded.

Irene Coleman had drilled everyone in the family repeatedly about this evening's protocol. Jonathan would go off on his own as soon as they arrived at Sixth and Smithfield—"some things I need to do," he had mumbled to his mother who at first started to protest before realizing that her son was nineteen years old and a working man, and didn't need to hold his mother's hand—and he most likely would come back home by himself so he could catch a few hours sleep before heading off again in the early morning hours to the Strip District and work.

Joseph also wanted to head off by himself but Irene objected, and Gerald sustained that objection with a slight compromise in recognition that his second son was almost an adult himself. The evening's remaining hours would be broken up into three blocks in which different stores would be covered. Until 7:00, the family would be in Gimbel's, where Joseph could head off by himself to parts of the store different than where the others would be or even out of the department store to surrounding shops, as long as he met up everyone else at 7:00 sharp at the corner of Sixth and Smithfield outside the store. The family would then trek down to Joseph Horne Company, where they would once again rendezvous at 8:00 at the Penn Avenue entrance after Joseph would head off on his own if he wanted. They would move back uptown to Kaufmann's Department Store, where at 8:15 Jonathan would meet up with the rest of them for hot cocoa and pie in the store's Tic Toc restaurant—a so-rare treat so special that even Jonathan wouldn't pass up. Joseph could then again head elsewhere if he wanted, but at exactly 9:45 he would meet up with the rest of the family underneath Kaufmann's landmark clock, where they would catch the streetcar that would take them back home, Ruthie no doubt falling asleep in her father's or mother's arms during the short, gently rocking ride.

The evening's primary shopping-related purpose was for the Coleman children to buy gifts for each other, as well as for Irene to pick up a few of the children's presents... but only a few. Since she and Gerald would have the youngest three split between them for most of the evening, Irene would have precious little time when she could buy gifts unobserved by at least one of the children. And since she couldn't trust any of them to keep a single gift-related secret from the others, Irene's shopping options were rather limited this evening.

However, the children would point or cast their eyes at potential presents throughout the evening's trek, and upon returning home Irene and Gerald could finalize their gift list once and for all. Tomorrow, Irene would head downtown by herself, retracing the family's steps among the department stores to pick up the rest of the gifts. Earlier in the day Irene had withdrawn $50 from the Coleman's Christmas Club account at the Dollar Savings Bank branch closest to their house and had divided the money equally with Gerald to cover the costs of the children's gifts for each other plus any gifts she was able to pick up tonight on the sly. Tomorrow she would return to the same bank branch and withdraw another $100 for the remaining purchases, plus her gift for Gerald (which she still hadn't decided on).

Long ago, in more affluent times before the Depression years, Irene's Christmas shopping also included presents for her own brothers and sisters and her own parents, as well as Gerald's own brothers, sister, and mother. But Gerald's mother and both of Irene's parents had passed away within months of each other in 1931 and other than her brother Stan, everyone else had long since departed from Pittsburgh, mostly in search of work during the early and mid-1930s in one coal mine or another across Pennsylvania or West Virginia. Money simply wasn't available during those years to continue the expanded Christmas gift giving, and the miles between Pittsburgh and where most of Gerald's and her own siblings had landed was a convenient excuse to halt the gift exchanges, which to date had never resumed. But with Stan and Lois still in Pittsburgh and living in the Coleman's house—an arrangement that was particularly awkward during the Christmas season—exceptions were made to include Stan, Lois, Marty, and Lorraine in the season's gift-giving. (Irene invariably slipped Stan a few bucks to cover the costs of presents that he and Lois would buy and Gerald knew about his wife's surreptitious money transfer, but he said nothing to spoil the small joys of the season).

From Ruth's point of view, the sole purpose of this evening's downtown sojourn was for her to finally be able to tell the real Santa at Kaufmann's and his helpers at Gimbel's and Horne's what she wanted for Christmas. For more than a week she was frantic that the delay in the family shopping trip would mean that her gift list wouldn't make it from downtown Pittsburgh to the North Pole in time for Santa to include her gifts this coming Wednesday on his Christmas Eve travels.

Don't worry, her mother had repeatedly assured her, Santa could take orders from little children as late as Wednesday afternoon—on Christmas Eve itself!—and still make sure that the presents would be delivered on time. Of course Ruthie knew that just because she sat on Santa's lap and the laps of Santa's helpers and gave them her wish list of gifts that she wouldn't receive everything on her list. Her parents had told her during the past few years, and reminded her again this year, how Santa sometimes had to take a few gifts off of every child's list so he could fit everything into his sleigh, but then he would try to make up for any shortfalls the following year.

After getting off the streetcar in front of Gimbel's, Ruthie excitedly pulled her mother's hand in the direction of the store's front door, and once in the store towards where she knew Santa's helper would be set up on his throne. Irene silently said a quick prayer that the line wouldn't be too long, and she was rewarded when she surprisingly only saw about ten children in line. Gerald headed off with Charlene and Thomas in tow to another part of the store after agreeing to rendezvous back with Irene and Ruthie in about twenty minutes.

("That's so Thomas can sit on Santa's lap, too," Charlene said, a bit more bite in her tone and her words than ordinary older sister-younger brother teasing would call for. But a single cold-eyed look from Gerald, first at Charlene and then at Thomas, cut off the bickering before it could even get started.)

When they all got back together—Joseph was still off somewhere, possibly still in Gimbel's or maybe elsewhere—the parents traded Charlene and Ruthie, and Irene and her older daughter headed off in the direction of women's clothing while Gerald took the other two to the toys and games department.

As Irene and Charlene passed the jewelry department, Irene suddenly turned on impulse to catch Charlene walking ever more slowly and staring at the display counter of engagement rings and wedding bands... staring with a sense of purpose, Irene was certain.

Charlene sensed Irene's gaze and quickly looked away from the rings as she continued walking, refusing to catch her mother's eyes.

❀ ❀ ❀

Outside Gimbel's, Joseph was leisurely strolling around the perimeter of the department store, pausing at each of the display windows. As was customary every year, the windows had been unveiled the day after Thanksgiving. However, the Pearl Harbor attack and the coming of war had sent the Gimbel Brothers' decorating staff into "Plan

B" at the direction of the store's management, who in turn were reacting to "do something patriotic!" orders from the company's management in New York. The windows were quickly blanketed to cut off the view from the sidewalks for two days before the hastily redone displays were once again unveiled.

The new result was a curious mix of Christmas-oriented and war-themed decorations: Santa and Uncle Sam together in one window display, handing out presents to little mannequin children dressed in Army combat uniforms. In another, Santa's sleigh was shown flying above an oversized globe with Europe and a large portion of the Pacific highlighted, and the Santa mannequin was dangling strung-together signs from the sleigh down to the globe, the signs bearing single words like "hope," "faith," "freedom," and "prayer." Yet another window showed little American children giving presents to Santa rather than the other way around, with indications that Santa would cross enemy lines and brave enemy fire to deliver their sacrificial gifts to the imprisoned children of continental Europe.

Joseph strolled through the snowflakes that had begun only moments earlier, from window to window, his mind distant. For the first time, he was coming to terms with his fate, courtesy of the curious mixture he saw in each window, a mixture of Santa and Uncle Sam, Christmas and war, his peaceful childhood and his uncertain future, and—though not explicitly shown in any Gimbel's window—life and death.

❀ ❀ ❀

Immediately after the rest of the family had disappeared from sight, Jonathan had hopped onto yet another streetcar and headed for the north side, not far from where his father had been earlier that day at the war plant. Jonathan's destination was the upscale Boggs and Buhl department store that catered primarily to those who lived on "millionaire's row" in the area known as Allegheny City. Jonathan wanted privacy while he purchased the engagement ring on which he had finally decided, and since probably half of Pittsburgh was crowded into downtown this evening, the chances of running into someone he or Francine knew were pretty high.

But Jonathan was fairly certain he wouldn't run into anyone from Polish Hill or Bloomfield or Lawrenceville at Boggs and Buhl, not only because of the upscale nature of the store but also because most Christmas shoppers opted for the same plan his own family did, trying to hit as many department stores (and Santa Clauses) in a few short hours as possible. And with the downtown department stores clustered so closely together—not just the ones to which Irene and Gerald were taking the rest of the family, but also Rosenbaum's and the one directly across from Kaufmann's, Frank and Seder's—those employing the same strategy used for Halloween trick-or-treating (as many homes in as little time as possible) wouldn't be spending precious minutes crossing the Allegheny River to where Jonathan was right now.

He had hesitated when he got off the streetcar in front of the store, he hesitated as soon as he went through the store's revolving door, and he hesitated yet once more as soon as the jewelry department came into sight. Somewhere deep inside the recesses of his mind, Jonathan was certain that what he was about to do was nothing more than a futile gesture, and indeed was an act of combined desperation and stupidity.

Still, Jonathan felt compelled to go through with the entire course of action: buying the ring and offering it to Francine with a marriage proposal... assuming he could finally find her to ask her, of course.

Going ahead with a flawed plan, most likely doomed to failure: good practice for what probably lay ahead for him on a battlefield in either Europe or some island in the Pacific, Jonathan thought, as he forced himself to resume walking towards the jewelry counter.

Just after 7:00, Irene and Gerald rounded up everyone near the front door of Gimbel's and began the short trek over to Horne's. Gerald immediately noticed Joseph wasn't saying much, but assumed the boy's silence was due to being a seventeen-year old boy dragged along on a shopping trip with his parents and younger siblings. Jonathan had been that way at the same age, the football star still being treated in many ways like he was a child.

Gerald watched Joseph while they walked and the boy wasn't looking in his father's direction. A wave of sadness washed over Gerald as he realized that this would be the last few hours that Joseph would ever spend time with his family in exactly this way. Even without the war only a few more years of shopping with his family would be the case for Joseph anyway, just as with Jonathan. Still, the times being what they were, the disintegration of the Coleman family as it now existed was being accelerated at a pace that anguished the family's patriarch.

The windows at Horne's were remarkably like those at Gimbel's, but this time Gerald walked around the store with Joseph while Irene ushered the other three inside, Ruthie of course heading directly to another Santa's helper. In one window three children were receiving gifts from Santa in the left half of the display and in the right half, depositing those same gifts in barrels that read "For Our Troops." Then, in the next window directly to the right, Santa was delivering those same presents to fatigue-clad mannequin troops, all of whom had very realistic-looking rifles slung over the shoulders and various weapons of other types—grenades, bazookas, and even a machine gun—scattered on the floor of the display.

Gerald and Joseph caught each other's eyes as they turned to head into the store, but neither said anything.

The parents knew that selecting a gift for Thomas would be easy enough, particularly this year. The youngest son was waiting for his brother and father, choosing not to wait in yet another Santa line with Ruthie, Charlene, and his mother. The Coleman men took the elevator to the sporting goods department on the fourth floor, and Thomas paused at the display of footballs. Thomas had gone out for freshmen football at Schenley, hoping to follow in his oldest brothers' footsteps. Whereas Jonathan had been the school's star player, Joseph—whose high school football career had ended the previous month—had never risen above second-string, with limited playing time and usually only in the final moments of games already won or lost.

Thomas often wondered which brother's path he would follow—Jonathan the star or Joseph the bench-warmer—and had made it very clear to his parents that with a football of his own with which to practice at home, he might also be a star like his oldest brother. So Irene and Gerald had already marked Thomas down for a football to accompany Thomas' other gift that Gerald was making by hand in his shop: a set of football cleats.

As Gerald watched both Joseph and Thomas wander over to a display of baseball gloves and excitedly try on one after another, an inspiration hit him for a gift for Joseph and also one more gift for Thomas. For three years now he had been using Jonathan's hand-me-down glove, Jonathan having received a new glove as a Christmas present in 1937 after making the varsity baseball team. Thomas still had to make due with a much-too-tight mid-1920s model that Gerald was able to keep in good repair through constant restitching, but which wouldn't do if Thomas also went out for the baseball team this coming spring as planned. New baseball gloves for both of them, Gerald thought; even though Joseph only has one more season left of high school baseball this coming spring, he could take his new glove with him and get into some games on board a Navy ship or at an Army base, wherever he wound up in the war. A new baseball glove would be a little touch of home when Joseph would be so far away...

"Come on, boys," Gerald finally said, confident that as they turned back in the direction of the elevator to take them to the bottom floor to meet up with Irene and the girls, Thomas walked away fairly certain that he would be receiving a new baseball glove in a few days but knew nothing about the cleats, while Joseph had no inkling that a new glove would be under the tree in a gift-wrapped package bearing his name.

❀ ❀ ❀

Charlene had once again slowed down and gaped at the engagement ring display counter in Horne's as she had done in Gimbel's, and once again Irene noticed. It was as if Charlene wished she could tell her mother about her secret engagement to Larry... not to provoke a confrontation or even just for her mother to know, but as if she wanted and needed her mother's advice on the matter.

Charlene found herself constantly thinking about Larry as she walked around the department store and along the downtown shops between them. She was, of course, trying to find the perfect gift for her brand-new fiancé: a scarf or a pair of winter gloves just wouldn't do it. She wondered what Larry would be buying her—again she thought that maybe, just maybe, he really would surprise her with an engagement ring, but couldn't help but feel cheated and a little worried if he indeed made that choice. Since she couldn't wear an engagement ring it would look as if Larry hadn't given her a Christmas gift at all... which would of course trigger immediate suspicion on the part of her all-knowing mother.

What kept coming back to Charlene over and over was the sensation—not just the memory, she could actually feel his touch as if he were right beside her, invisible to all—of

Larry's fingers teasing her. She knew what would come next in the natural progression and one part of her wanted that to happen, while another part of her was still very much a young girl, confused and wondering if Larry was simply taking liberties with her only to laughingly discard her in the not-too-distant future, as teenage boys often did.

She looked over at her mother, somehow feeling that her mother would have the answers, but she didn't dare ask. Irene Coleman hadn't been one for soul-baring mother-daughter talks, least so far, and Charlene assumed her mother was waiting for that "wedding night talk" occasion... which could very possibly be too late. Charlene sometimes wondered what her mother, exhausted as Irene always was from her endless schedule of household chores and child-rearing, had been like when she had been Charlene's age. Irene never volunteered any information other than an occasional sudden—and superficial—"when I was your age" reminisce in the middle of some task or another.

"Let's go to the men's department," Charlene suddenly said to her mother, "I decided what I want to buy for Larry." An inspiration had hit her; maybe a matching set of cufflinks, tie pin, and collar stick wasn't "the perfect" gift but it was, Charlene thought, appropriate enough for a secret fiancé.

❀ ❀ ❀

The Horne's portion of the evening's journey was completed exactly at 8:00 (as if anyone in the Coleman family had any doubt that Irene would keep everyone precisely on schedule), and as they began walking back towards Kaufmann's they realized that the snowfall was much heavier than it had been an hour earlier, now covering the pavement to the point where the thousands of footsteps no longer bore down to slushy pavement but instead compacted the snow into an endless solid gray-and-white mass along the length of every sidewalk. Gerald lifted Ruthie to carry her and prevent the little girl from slipping on the slick snow-covered sidewalks (or having someone slip and fall into her). Irene almost reached to grasp Thomas' hand as they walked along before remembering that he was fourteen and would die of embarrassment if one of his friends came across him holding his mother's hand. Instead she conversed with Charlene, who suddenly had become more talkative and in a more lighthearted mood than earlier in the evening. Likewise, Joseph seemed to snap out of his funk and he and Thomas lagged slightly behind the others, talking about football and baseball, game days past and hopeful days of glory ahead.

Just as they were crossing Wood Street, a block away from Kaufmann's, Jonathan suddenly materialized, punching Joseph lightly in the arm and wrapping a headlock around Thomas' head for a split second before releasing his grip. Like Joseph and Charlene, he was more chipper than he had been earlier in the evening; both his parents assumed that whatever the cause for his moodiness had been overtaken by the evening filled with Christmas window displays, the gentle snowfall, and the bustle of people all over downtown who refused to acknowledge the uncertainty and fear of the war, at least for a few precious hours.

Irene led them into the Tic Toc restaurant where they spotted only one circular table open in the entire restaurant, in the back near the kitchen door, that still appeared slightly too small for the entire family. Both Gerald and Irene scanned the counter but didn't see more than two seats together anywhere, and perhaps only five unoccupied seats in total. So the hostess ushered them to the one open table and pulled up two extra chairs, and they all crowded around, Ruthie sitting on her mother's lap. The waitress quickly came over—she knew that most of her customers this time of evening wanted to eat and get out of the restaurant as quickly as possible to squeeze in that last shopping run—bringing a pot of coffee with her from which she poured steaming cups for the parents, who indicated that each of the children—including Jonathan—wanted hot cocoa. Nearly everyone in the family ordered hot apple pie except for Irene and Charlene, who instead opted for slices of the coconut custard pie that Irene always claimed "Tic Toc was famous for."

The coffee, cocoa and pie were consumed as quickly as dinner earlier that evening, and by 8:40 the evening's shopping entered the home stretch, urged along by Ruthie who would finally get to sit on the lap of the *real* Santa Claus, the one at Kaufmann's, not his helpers in the other stores earlier in the evening.

Ruthie waited patiently in line for her turn, and then climbed the four steps to the platform and was helped onto Santa's lap by her mother, who accompanied her. She ran through the same list that she had given twice before earlier that evening: a doll and clothes for the doll, coloring books and crayons, a bicycle. Irene had already purchased all of Ruthie's gifts except the bicycle at the Grant's 5 and

10 store, and the presents were already wrapped and stashed safely in a locked trunk in the Colemans' attic. The bicycle was still up in the air, though; a new bicycle would cost at least $20, and until she and Gerald had a better idea of the complete list of gifts for the rest of the children Irene wasn't sure if they would be able to afford the bicycle.

Still, as she watched Ruthie's eyes light up when she described the bike she wanted in detail to Santa—the pink color, the bell on the left handlebar just above the handgrip, the multi-colored streamers dropping from both handlebars—she was determined that if at all possible she'd have a bicycle, tied with a big pink bow, propped up against the dining room wall next to the Christmas tree.

Ruthie indeed fell asleep in her father's arms on the streetcar, and she never fully awoke as Irene took off the little girl's boots and coat, hat and gloves, scarf and sweater. She carried Ruthie up to her room and finished undressing her and then helping the girl into her pajamas, and tucking her in with a goodnight kiss. Irene thought she saw—though maybe she was imagining—a genuine smile on Ruthie's face as she drifted back into sleep, no doubt relieved that she had finally gotten to connect with Santa after nearly two weeks of delay.

Thomas' normal 10:00 bedtime was extended a half hour since he didn't have school and both parents knew that the boy was still keyed up from walking through the brisk cold and from the excitement of shopping. He flipped on the radio at five minutes after ten in time to catch NBC

Radio's *News Here and Abroad* program. The newscaster announced that Churchill was now in Washington to meet with President Roosevelt, apparently having successfully dodged U-boats all the way across the Atlantic. Gerald, settling into his chair just as the news report was being broadcast, thought that now that the Germans knew Churchill was in America and would have to head back to Britain at some point in the not-too-distant future, getting back home safely might be quite another matter.

The rest of the news was a mixture of war news from Europe, Africa, and the Pacific—nothing really new since what had been reported in the afternoon *Pittsburgh Sun-Telegraph*—as well as Home Front news of solidifying rationing plans for food, all kinds of metal, gasoline and oil, and pretty much everything else. Most of the plans wouldn't be finalized until after New Year's but it seemed to Gerald that the government was slowly preparing people for what was coming, rather than just coming out and enacting various types of rationing that would immediately go into effect.

The news ended, Thomas was ushered off to bed as was Charlene, and Joseph was the last holdout still in the living room. (Jonathan had arrived home shortly after everyone else did, listened to two minutes of news, and then headed to his room to get as much sleep as he could before having to awaken in the frigid blackness at 2:45 so he could make it to work by 3:30.) Xavier Cugat's NBC show was up next and Joseph tried to roll the dial to catch the rebroadcast on CBS of Fred Allen's *Texaco Star Theater*, but the glare from Gerald caused Joseph to pull his hand away. Joseph didn't like Xavier Cugat or any other band leader's show, even Tommy Dorsey and Benny

Goodman and Glenn Miller, whom Jonathan occasionally tried to convince his brother were actually pretty good if you listened to the music and, more importantly, had a pretty girl to dance with (but Joseph wasn't having any part of this and wondered why his brother was suddenly acting so goofy).

Joseph gave up and headed off to his room—which is what Gerald wanted, he wasn't that fond of Xavier Cugat himself—leaving the parents as the last two downstairs in the house. Gerald rose out of his chair, turning the radio's volume down enough so he and Irene could hear if any one of the children sneaked downstairs to eavesdrop on them—and went into the kitchen, where Irene was pouring steaming cups of coffee for each of them.

They spent the next half hour comparing their mental lists that they had each compiled throughout the evening's shopping and settled on their final choices after adding up the prices of each present to make sure they would stay within the strict limits of their gift budget. The football, cleats, and baseball glove for Thomas; the baseball glove, flannel shirts, and winter boots (another gift being handmade by Gerald) for Joseph; the doll and doll clothes, coloring books and crayons, and—yes, they decided they could afford it—the bicycle for Ruthie; clothes and a new winter coat (which was desperately needed) for Charlene; and work clothes and another set of handmade boots for Jonathan.

The children's gifts decided, Gerald finally was able to discuss the two war plant job offers he had received earlier that day with his wife. He had told her bits and pieces throughout the late afternoon when he got home and on the streetcars to and from downtown, but between their children's presence—both keeping an eye on the younger ones as well as not wanting to say too much about the jobs in front of any of them—he hadn't yet had the opportunity to fully discuss the situation with Irene.

He reiterated what he had already told her earlier, about being sent from the north side plant to Mt. Washington, and how he had decided to accept the higher-paying supervisor's job in a profession that he already knew. He explained how on the one hand, making tanks seemed to have more of a direct relationship to the war effort than shoes and boots, but taking everything into account he figured that someone had to be a supervisor at the plant up on Mt. Washington to make footwear for the soldiers and sailors, so it might as well be someone like himself who knew the profession intimately and wouldn't stand for any slip-shod work by any of the workers there.

Irene listened to his explanation, occasionally nodding or offering an "um-hmm" in acknowledgment, and when he finished she offered the only commentary that she could think of.

"I'm just worried that you'll be exhausted between working in the plant and still doing your own work in the shop in the evenings," Irene said. She didn't offer one more concern of a personal nature, that most of the evenings Gerald had once spent at home would now be spent at his shop. And, with Jonathan most likely gone soon and Joseph soon thereafter, the house would seem so strangely empty in the evenings without the three of them there.

But Irene didn't voice that particular concern; she could make sacrifices and be a trooper, too, all for the cause. Gerald felt so strongly that he needed to do what he soon would do; why add to his burdens?

"And what are you getting me for Christmas?" Irene teasingly asked Gerald, changing the subject.

A smile finally came to his face as he sipped his coffee and just chuckled.

"You really want to know?" he asked her, knowing the answer.

"No," Irene shook her head, also smiling. More than anything, she was smiling because just like last year, the two of them could actually afford to buy more than a token present for each other now that the lean years were behind them. Neither knew if the war would soon bring back those same lean years of the 1930s—or perhaps even worse-off years, which was quite possible if the war continued to go so poorly—so conceivably this might be the last year in which a little bit of extravagance made an appearance in Gerald and Irene's gifts for each other.

Still, jewelry and frilly dresses were nowhere on her own wish list, Irene thought as they finished the last of their coffee, shut the lights in the kitchen and the living room, turned off the radio, and headed up the stairs (after Irene adjusted the radiator's heat just a tad lower; after all, every little bit helped). What she really wanted was that new bathrobe to replace the tattered one she was now putting on over her nightgown before walking over to embrace her husband, signaling her desire to cap such a wonderful evening by making this one of those infrequent nights when the two of them intimately came together.

Maybe he'll notice how shabby my robe is, she thought to herself as Gerald's hands came to rest on her shoulders for an instant before sliding down over the top part of her back to pull her towards him.

3—Tuesday, December 23, 1941

Jonathan Coleman grimaced as he grabbed his coffee mug with his left hand, those fingers—as well as those on his right hand—stiff and painful from more than an hour's work outside in temperatures barely above ten degrees. The morning ritual at *J. Weisberg & Sons* included several hours of loading the store's two flatbeds with boxes from the railroad cars that began arriving at 3:00 A.M. all along the strip district. The deals were made and Jonathan and the other workers would grab the boxes of lettuce and celery and apples and whatever else was being shipped into Pittsburgh from points far south and far west, and then unload those same boxes back in the store's warehouse area. Some of the boxes would then be carried or moved en mass with a handtruck to the store's customer area where throughout the day, people from all over Pittsburgh would come to buy their vegetables and fruit. Still more boxes remained in cold storage to be driven to restaurant and grocery market customers—those that didn't buy their own produce directly off of the trains, which many of the larger stores and restaurants did.

Old Man Weisberg's sons were either already off to the Army or Navy or would soon be on their way, which made workers like Jonathan even more valuable for as long as they'd be around until they themselves headed off to the war. Jonathan wondered what Old Man Weisberg would do then—probably have to hire a bunch of 4F workers, but would they be able to carry thousands of total pounds each day in the frigid cold or, when the next summer came around, in unbearable heat and humidity?

Oh well, Jonathan thought as he could only sip the coffee because of the steam rising from the black liquid; that's not my problem, once I'm away myself. He glanced at the clock—only 5:30 in the morning, still dark for almost two more hours—and wrapped the fingers of his right hand around the perimeter of the piping hot mug, hoping that the heat from the liquid inside would unstiffen his fingers. After about thirty seconds—all that he could stand, the mug was so hot—he switched the mug into his right hand, those fingers now feeling looser and less painful, and repeated the heat therapy ritual with the fingers from his left hand.

Alone for a minute, Jonathan found himself thinking about the reports that had begun filtering back from Europe, the stories about what the Germans were doing to the Jews there. Old Man Weisberg and his sons were Jews and several of Jonathan's co-workers—friends of Weisberg's sons—were as well, and Jonathan could never understand just what was with the Nazis. The stories about what had been going on in Germany itself had, of course, been known for several years... the reports of burning synagogues and rounding up the Jews, with the police just standing by; all of that. Now, more tales were surfacing that the Nazis were doing the same thing to Jews in the countries they had conquered: Poland, Austria, France, and all the rest.

No wonder the Old Man's sons are all going into the Army and Navy, Jonathan thought; if the Germans somehow invaded and conquered England and then turned their attention here, they would probably try to do the same thing to Jews in America, including Old Man Weisberg and his family.

Try as he might, Jonathan couldn't understand at all why the Nazis were doing what they were doing... assuming the stories were accurate, of course. At Schenley High Jonathan had gone to school and even played football with lots of Jews, mostly those who lived on the Hill—as Pittsburgh's Hill District was known. He had played football and baseball against other Jews from the mostly Jewish Squirrel Hill who went to Taylor Allderdice. Even the Detroit Tigers' Hank Greenberg, who had almost broken Babe Ruth's home run record, was Jewish.

As far as Jonathan could tell, Jews were just like everyone else here in America, except they went to synagogues instead of churches, and on Saturday instead of Sunday. Maybe things were different in Germany and elsewhere in Europe, but Jonathan couldn't see how. He turned his head to see two of Weisberg's sons walking towards him—actually, walking towards the coffee, so Jonathan took a small step to his left to give them room—and as he watched them flex their stiff fingers, their cheeks and noses bright red from the cold, puffs like miniature clouds appearing with each breath they exhaled from their noses and mouths—Jonathan imagined that right this very second a squad of black-clad Nazi S.S. stormtroopers barged into the warehouse area yelling "Jüden heraus!" (a phrase Jonathan knew from the increasing number of movies he saw with Francine in the past two years, films that walked the line between propaganda, information, and entertainment), submachine guns at the ready, and for no other reason than the two of them being Jewish, dragging them both away to some unknown fate. And, quite possibly, dragging Jonathan along simply because he chose to work alongside and consort with two Jews.

No, Jonathan couldn't imagine that happening at all; the entire scenario was so ludicrous and unbelievable, yet across Europe it actually was happening all over.

Something to think about, Jonathan thought as the two Weisberg boys finished their quick coffee and headed back into the frozen December morning blackness; something to think about.

Gerald Coleman was getting by on only four hours of sleep. His one-day "vacation" from the shop (two days if he wanted to count Sunday at church and later at Stan's and Lois') was as costly as he knew it would be. He had his typical backlog of repair work from his regular customers, many of whom wanted their shoes and boots back before Christmas Day. He had the football cleats to make for Thomas and two pairs of boots for Jonathan and Joseph, and the clock was running on those also since they needed to be sitting in wrapped packages underneath the family's Christmas tree by tomorrow night. Fortunately he was almost done with all three sets of footwear, and when he individually thought of any of the pairs of shoes and boots for his family and everyone else, all seemed to be in hand. However, when he thought of his waiting workload in his entirety, it all seemed overwhelming.

And now, as he threaded one of his toughest leather needles to stitch the roughly cut soles onto all four of the boots (two left-footed, two right-footed) for his sons, Gerald once again second-guessed his war plant decision. The sheer number of hours he would soon be working—at least 70 each week by his calculation, 40 at the plant and around 30 more spread out over evenings and Saturdays for his own business—would be as bone-wearying as anything he had ever done in his life.

No matter, Gerald thought to himself as he thrust the needle with added emphasis into the leather, yanking the needle and its attached stitching with the anger that had suddenly collected in his right arm and hand. Anger at himself, for putting himself in this situation mostly on impulse in reaction to Stan Walker's chatter two days earlier. Anger at John Grassi for sending him up to Mount Washington. Anger at Danny Harnchevik for offering him the job and still more anger at himself for accepting the job.

But Gerald Coleman was astute enough to reserve some anger for those who really deserved his fury: Tojo and Hitler, and Mussolini too, for setting all of this in motion in the first place.

If Charlene Coleman had realized what a poor keeper of secrets Lorraine Walker was, she would have picked someone else to tell about Larry and her. But Charlene had so desperately wanted to share the news of her engagement and her cousin was a confidant of long standing, so sharing one more secret with Lorraine seemed the right decision at the time. However, Charlene might just have well directly confided in her mother, because in less than 48 hours the result was the same.

Lois Walker dragged Lorraine with her to the market shortly after 8:30 that morning—against the girl's protests, since Lorraine wanted to spend a few extra precious hours in bed with no school that day, but Lois Walker wasn't having any more of that idea than her sister-in-law was with her own children. Inside the store they split up, Lois heading to the counter to get their order filled from the items that Mr. Wojzwoski kept out of his customers' reach, mostly out of custom. Lorraine walked up and down the four aisles filling a small basket with other items—three tins of sardines, a box of corn flakes, a can of baking powder—from the list her mother insisted she carry.

Right in front of the baking soda Lorraine ran into Harriet Brzonsky, a classmate of hers who also had an older sister—Molly—who was in the same class as Charlene. The two girls started talking as they slowly strolled the aisles, gossiping as if they hadn't seen each other for months or even years instead of a mere four days since their last school day before their Christmas recess.

"I know a secret," Harriet said in almost exactly the same tone Charlene had used when confiding in Lorraine two days earlier. She proceeded to tell Lorraine what she had heard from her sister about one of Molly's and Lorraine's classmates who was "in trouble."

"She might have to get married and she just turned seventeen," Harriet exclaimed.

Not to be outdone, Lorraine countered with a secret that she happened to know, but wasn't quite so conscientious about lowering her voice when she told Harriet about Charlene and Larry Moncheck. And, as fate would have it, Lois Walker happened to be exactly opposite the two girls at that very moment, in the next aisle over but well within earshot.

Lois Walker said nothing to her daughter about what she had overheard, but when they left the market she slightly altered their morning plans.

"I'll take these groceries home," she indicated the one paper bag in her arms and the other in Lorraine's, "if you go to the bakery and pick up two loaves of bread and then come right back home."

Lorraine didn't think too much of this change in plans and simply handed the grocery bag (which had been the heavier of the two, anyway) to her mother and accepted a half dollar in exchange to pay for the bread.

"Don't forget to bring me back the change," Lois warned, but Lorraine wouldn't have dared splurge with the leftover 34 cents; on candy or lipstick or anything. Ever since Stan Walker had gone back to work after being without a job for so many years, Lois had warned Marty and Lorraine that just because money was coming into the family and they now had a house of their own once again, no one knew what the future held, and every spare penny was to be saved "just in case."

Lorraine headed off to the bakery and Lois headed for home, quickly, and as soon as she walked in the back door of the house to the kitchen she set the grocery bags on the table and dialed her sister-in-law's phone number without even pausing to unpack the bags.

Irene answered in the middle of the second ring. She had just finished the breakfast dishes and wanted to get through the morning's dusting and sweeping as quickly as possible so she could go to the bank, withdraw the additional money from the Christmas Club account, and make her rounds of the downtown stores to buy the remaining presents. Joseph and Thomas had been drafted into grocery and bakery detail, with Charlene ordered to stay home to watch Ruthie until Irene returned from downtown, probably around 3:00 that afternoon.

"Hello?"

"Irene, it's Lois."

A bit of irritation swept over Irene. Lois should be doing the same things that morning as Irene was, and shouldn't have time to call her sister-in-law for some idle chatter.

"Hello Lois, I was just finishing up the dishes and getting to the cleaning so I can get to downtown to do the Christmas shopping." Maybe Lois would take the hint that Irene was very, very busy and pressed for time and would keep this call short.

Lois got right down to business.

"I overheard something this morning that I thought you should know," she said, pausing for her sister-in-law's reaction.

All kinds of wild ideas flashed through Irene's mind, but among those ideas was not what Lois said in response to Irene's cautious "What?"

"Lorraine told Harriet Brzonsky that Charlene and Larry Moncheck are secretly engaged."

Silence. Shock. More silence. Absolutely no words coming from Irene's side of the phone call.

"Irene?"

More silence, then finally:

"I heard." Words said dispassionately, evenly, as if what she had just heard was entirely expected.

"Well?" Lois asked anxiously.

Well what? What did she expect Irene to say or do? Ask her sister-in-law to repeat what she had said, because Irene couldn't have possibly heard her correctly? Demand that Lois immediately retract what she had said, as if it couldn't possibly be true, how could she be spreading such horribly untrue gossip? Perhaps an anguished wail, or a cry of "Oh God, how could she do this to me?"

"I've got to go," was all Irene said, then she added,

"Lois, do me a favor? Don't say anything about this to anyone else?"

"I won't," Lois promised, but since Lorraine had inherited her lack of discretion from her mother, Irene couldn't be sure that Lois would keep her promise.

No matter, though; Irene suddenly had other worries than what Lois did or didn't say to anyone else, and besides, she wouldn't be saying anything that was untrue or that could harm her daughter's reputation, anyway. It wasn't as if Lois was reporting that Lorraine had told Harriet Brzonsky that Charlene was pregnant and...

Now, a cold sweat broke out instantaneously all over Irene's body. Was that why Charlene, not even seventeen years old, was engaged? Was she planning on eloping and running away with Larry to some place where they could be married so her baby wouldn't be born amidst public sin?

The panic subsided after a few seconds, and Irene— whose instincts seemed to be quite on the mark, at least most of the time—was fairly sure that this secret engagement was not because her daughter was pregnant, and in fact was somehow tied to her daughter *not* giving in to any pressure from Larry.

At that moment Charlene walked from the living room into the kitchen, heading to the icebox.

"Ruthie wants a glass of milk, is that OK?" she asked her mother.

"Certainly, but she needs to drink it in here so she doesn't spill it in the living room. Pour it out for her and then tell her to come in here."

Irene's words and tone: perfectly normal and natural, as if the conversation that had begun a minute and a half earlier and ended barely thirty seconds ago had never occurred. She would get to the bottom of this soon enough; no use tipping her hand until she knew what cards she was going to play.

❀ ❀ ❀

Ten o'clock; no putting it off any longer.

Jonathan Coleman stuck his head into the front of the store to ask Old Man Weisberg if he could make a quick phone call, that he had skipped his last break so he wouldn't be cheating the old man out of ten minutes or so of work.

"Go ahead, make it snappy," came back the Russian-accented reply.

Jonathan grabbed his coat and shuffled through the crusted, packed snow to the pay phone on Smallman Street, the same phone where twice the previous day Jonathan had encountered an unyielding defense—in the form of Mrs. Donner—that was peer to any against which he had played on the Schenley football team. He fully expected Mrs. Donner again, and had angrily sworn to himself that if the result of this phone call was the same those of the previous day, then Francine could just go to hell, he wouldn't call her any more, that (since he was thinking in football terms) the final whistle had blown on the Jonathan-Francine romance... the clock had run out.

He grimaced at the instant bite of the cold as he pulled the glove off of his right hand to reach into his pants pocket for a nickel. He dropped the nickel into the phone's coin slot, dialed Francine's number, and then cradled the handset between his head and left shoulder as put his right glove back onto his suddenly very cold right hand.

Two rings, and then:

"Hello?"

For an uncomfortably long second, Jonathan was too stunned to speak. He had prepared himself, steeled himself for Mrs. Donner's voice and now that Francine had answered the phone, the talk-to-her-mother script in his mind went flying away and he was at a loss for words.

Finally, he recovered.

"Hi Francine, it's Jonathan." Pause... pause... now what?

"Hi, sweetie!" Bubbly, almost sugary tones.

"Um... hi." Decision time: should Jonathan say anything about how he had tried three times to reach her yesterday? Ask her where she was all day? Mention that he hadn't spoken with Francine for an entire week, since the previous Tuesday when she had broken the news about her date with Donnie?

"I'm sorry I missed your calls yesterday," Francine picked up the slack in the conversation and taking away one of Jonathan's possible questions. "I was doing my

Christmas shopping and didn't get home until dinner time." Another of Jonathan's questions down.

"I went shopping with my family last night," Jonathan said cautiously, "that's why I didn't try to call you anymore yesterday."

Should he continue? Why not?

"Besides," Jonathan said, "I think your mother and father didn't sound too happy that I called three times."

"Oh, don't worry about them," Francine answered, the volume of her voice dropping a bit as if she didn't want to be overheard, "my mom is grumpy because of all the work she's doing getting ready for Christmas, and my dad keeps complaining about all the money he's spending."

"I figured it was something like that," Jonathan answered. So what was the harm in a little white lie?

"So when do I get my Christmas present?" Francine asked, her voice again syrupy. "I have yours all ready for you, wrapped and everything."

"Um, how about tomorrow, Christmas Eve?" Jonathan blurted out, at the same time realizing that his mother would kill him if he didn't go to church with his family and then spend the evening at home.

"OK, but it will have to be sometime in the afternoon, my mom is planning this big family to-do, you know, church and then all of us spending the evening together..."

"Mine too!" Jonathan interrupted, and for the first time in the conversation he was at ease. So... apparently all his fears had been for naught, just a touch of paranoia no doubt heightened by everything else going on around them. So what if she had gone out with Donnie Yablonski? Donnie would be gone in a couple days and here was Francine, on the phone with Jonathan this very instant, making plans to exchange Christmas gifts on Christmas Eve. Someday, after they were married, he would confide in her about how unsettled he had been for one entire week near the end of December, 1941, but that all had turned out well for Jonathan and Francine Coleman.

"How about if I come over to your house at 4:30 tomorrow, then?" Jonathan offered and as Francine agreed to the time and location, Jonathan was thankful that he had followed through with his plan to buy her the engagement ring the night before, instead of doing what every thought and impulse in his head had urged him to do: turn around and walk out of Boggs and Buhl, the $145 still in his pocket and the ring still in the display case.

"I can't wait to see you" was how Francine ended her part of the conversation and Jonathan had to fight off the impulse to reply "I love you." He didn't want the very first time he said those words to Francine Donner to be over the telephone on a Tuesday morning, her at home and Jonathan standing out in the freezing December weather, the wind whipping frozen crystals that stung his face. He'd tell her tomorrow when he handed her the ring, sitting by the fire in her living room as the winter sun slowly faded outside—if her parents would give them some privacy—and all would be right, at least in that little small corner of their world.

Gerald Coleman rolled the dial on the radio in his shop, trying to find something other than war news. The same reports that he had heard last night—the Japanese invasion of Luzon in the Philippines, Churchill's conference with Roosevelt—were being related by the NBC, Liberty, and Mutual networks; everywhere Gerald let the dial rest. Gerald just wanted to listen to some soothing Christmas music—carols or contemporary, he didn't much care—rather than the same old war news... or, worse, *new* war news which no doubt wouldn't be good.

He found KDKA halfway through *Silent Night*, which then gave way to *Oh Holy Night*, and then a commercial break for Camel followed by another one for Lucky Strikes... which reminded Gerald, he really could use a smoke (one of the downsides of his trade, both hands needing to be engaged most of the time), and he'd take a cigarette break shortly. Gerald's fingers continued working automatically once back at the needle and thread, only requiring an occasional beaconing glance of his eyes to keep the needle on track as he continued working on Jonathan's boots. The announcer came back after the commercial and informed his listening audience that the next group of songs wouldn't be Christmas music, but rather a collection of recently released war songs.

First up was Carson Robison singing *Remember Pearl Harbor*, which was followed by a different song with the same title, this one sung by Sammy Kaye. Next came *We Did It Before And We'll Do It Again*, sung by Dick Robertson and, according to the announcer, recorded just a week earlier and rushed to the awaiting, demanding American public. Gerald was struck by the common tone and theme of both of these songs: sure, the enemy struck first and drew first blood but they have no idea what they started; *we'll* be the ones finishing the job! What really troubled Gerald was the absolute certainty in the message of the songs: we *will* win, things couldn't possibly turn out any other way!

The next song was more of the same: Teddy Powell singing *Goodbye, Mama (I'm Off To Yokohama)*, which was followed by yet another thematically identical song: *Let's Put The Axe To The Axis*, sung by Abe Lyman.

Propaganda: that's what this all is, the thought suddenly came to Gerald: simple propaganda. All of these songs had been written, recorded, and distributed within the past couple of weeks as the war was unfolding, seemingly in lockstep with the news from the war fronts. But why wasn't there a song about the Wehrmacht poised outside of Moscow, or U-boats sinking British and American merchant ships by the dozens in the frigid North Atlantic? If there was a song about the Japanese attack on Pearl Harbor, why not another musical ditty about the Japanese invasion of the Philippines that was happening this very moment, and another with rhyming lyrics describing their assault on Wake Island?

Carson Robison made another appearance; apparently his version of *Remember Pearl Harbor* wasn't enough of a contribution to the war effort, so now Gerald found himself listening to *We're Gonna Have To Slap The Dirty Little Jap (And Uncle Sam's The Guy Who Can Do It)*. Halfway through the song Gerald flicked the dial with fury in his fingers, the radio tuner halting on the opening notes of *Jingle Bells*.

What kind of music would be played on American radios next Christmas, Gerald wondered? The same "don't think about how badly things are going, we're *still* going to win this war!" feel-good propaganda? Would the war still even be going next year at this time, or will it already have been lost?

Jingle Bells was followed by the news, but just as Gerald was starting to flick the dial again to avoid the war news, he stopped. An air raid drill would be held Friday, the day after Christmas, at noon, the announcer said; spread the word so everyone in Pittsburgh would know that it wouldn't be a genuine German attack from the air. And apparently a major point of controversy, according to the radio announcer as he moved on to the next story, was the mechanism through which rationing would soon be implemented: books of coupons versus books of stamps. The announcer didn't specifically state the details of the controversy but Gerald assumed counterfeiting was a concern; however he quite honestly didn't know which method would be less susceptible to black market profiteering.

Finally, he just flicked off the radio's power; enough news, enough war songs. A quick Pall Mall, maybe two, and then it was back to work on his children's Christmas gifts. He needed to finish in enough time to take the streetcar to Grant's to buy Ruthie's bicycle, the only one of the children's gifts that he wouldn't be making by hand nor would Irene be buying this afternoon.

❀ ❀ ❀

Irene Coleman's God-given ability to do two, three, or even four things at the same time without breaking stride—or maybe it was an acquired talent, but regardless the result was the same—came in handy that afternoon as she glided from one department store to another, and within each store from one department to another, rapidly dwindling down the number of unfilled items on her Christmas gift list. Even as she picked out the gifts, counted out cash, and waited in line for the free gift-wrapping, her mind dwelled on her predicament caused by the sudden news about Charlene. She went over and over and over and over the situation, but couldn't reconcile the conflicting emotions she felt.

As Charlene's mother—the mother of a sixteen-year old high school junior—she was appalled at her daughter being engaged; secretly or openly, it made no difference. Going steady with Larry Moncheck was one thing, and like any good Polish mother anywhere in Pittsburgh, Irene hoped and prayed that her daughter landed a good husband... but *after* she finished high school, not before. Or, at worst, Irene could come to terms with her daughter becoming engaged sometime in the closing months of her high school years, graduation right around the corner. But at this age, a year and a half away from graduation? Far, far too soon. Worse, if Charlene was pregnant, the girl might have no choice; Irene just didn't know.

Yet aside from Charlene's situation, Lois Walker's news had catalyzed a stirring deep inside Irene, something that she hadn't felt in close to 25 years. Even as Irene's eyes took in the downtown Pittsburgh street scenes, the store displays, the faces of the sales people to whom she handed the precious paper money in exchange for the gifts that she prayed would make her children's Christmas, 1941 a memorable one, she could also clearly gaze upon an unbelievably young Irene Walker—younger than Charlene was now, eleven, maybe twelve years old.

As a young girl growing up in Pittsburgh, in that brief period of peace and growing prosperity after the Spanish-American War and before America entered The Great War, Irene Walker had had dreams... many dreams, delicious dreams. She had been a ferocious reader as a young girl, reading every novel that she found around her parents' modest house or that she could borrow from a neighbor or the small neighborhood lending library. *Dorothy Vernon of Haddon Hall*, Alice Caldwell Hegan's *Mrs. Wiggs of the Cabbage Patch*, Mary Augusta Ward's *Lady Rose's Daughter*; Irene loved novels about parts of America she had only heard about and dreamed of someday seeing, and novels about other exotic parts of the world. She had read everything she could find by Winston Churchill—she smiled, thinking about the now-all-but-forgotten novelist whose very name had been eclipsed by his British namesake in whom Britain's last hopes rested. *The Crossing, Coniston, Mr. Crewe's Career...* Churchill's books came back to her in memories she hadn't thought about for years.

Irene had lost herself in stories like *Rebecca of Sunnybrook Farm* and tales of the romanticized Gilded Age, like Edith Wharton's *The House of Mirth*. She particularly loved stories about make-believe places such as George Barr McCutcheon's *Truxton King*. While she was reading, and in the immediate aftermath, Irene Walker could see herself as many of the characters whose tales she took in. She could be the wife of a Gilded Age industrial captain, or even the wife of a horse-breeder, or the wife of a career foreign service diplomat, spending her life in those same exotic foreign locations she read about: Australia, New Zealand, Singapore, Hong Kong... some of which were now about to fall any day to the Army and Navy of the Japanese Empire, Irene suddenly realized with a shudder. Other places she had also dreamed about—France, in particular, but also her ancestral homeland of Poland that she wanted to someday see in person—had already fallen to Hitler.

As she did so often during the past weeks Irene forced the sudden intruding thoughts of the war from her head. She couldn't do anything about Tojo's designs on Hong Kong or Singapore, or what Hitler was now doing in France and Belgium and Austria. She could, however, do something about her daughter and this sudden news of a secret engagement to a boy—and Larry Moncheck *was* just a boy—who would soon be fighting to free one or the other of those places Irene Walker had dreamed about long ago.

Her thoughts again drifted back to 1912, 1913... she saw herself as she actually once was, as a young girl who was certain that there was a future better for her somewhere else in the world than the one that would be hers if she did as her immigrant parents hoped for her: stay in high school long enough to land a husband from somewhere in the neighborhood and then become the mother that her own mother had become, and her mother's mother before, and...

Irene's mother had had her eye on Gerald Coleman, the boy from four houses down the street, since 1912, when Gerald was barely fourteen and Irene, lost in her novels, had been only eleven years old herself. Fannie Walker and Natasha Coleman conspired and plotted that the two would become betrothed as if they were old-country matchmakers or marriage brokers. Irene initially showed no interest in Gerald Coleman; he was, after all, a boy three years older than her, which meant the two had absolutely nothing in common when their respective mothers initially began encouraging them to spend time together. Gerald was pleasantly handsome enough, but he was always so... serious, that's how Irene thought of him. She saw herself someday marrying a debonair, aristocratic who would be received at the best homes in New York City and Boston and London and Paris; not a common shoemaker-in-the-making apprenticed to his father, his destiny already decided during his boyhood, before he even entered high school. Irene could picture herself being squired about town in a brand-new, custom-built Du Pont motor car, not the aging, mass-produced Model T that her father owned. Never could she have pictured herself twenty-five years later with a husband who didn't even own a car, her family's mode of transportation limited to streetcars and walking.

Ironically, The Great War did take Gerald Coleman to Europe, but his journey through Belgium and France as a rear echelon soldier was nothing even close to Irene's aspirations for The Continent. And the destruction that the war brought all over Europe cast a pall over Irene's girlhood dreams of foreign travel and adventure, which began to fade as she turned eighteen and Gerald came back from the Army and from Europe. For the first time, Irene Walker began to seriously consider her mother's plans for Gerald Coleman as her husband. He began courting her, and—ironically enough—on Christmas Day, 1919, Gerald proposed marriage to Irene Walker, who accepted. They put off the marriage until Gerald took over his father's cobbler business in early 1921, and were married that May.

All during her engagement, Irene second-guessed her decision, second-guessed surrendering her girlhood dreams of elegance and travel and excitement for all eternity. Gerald Coleman would no doubt be a dutiful husband and a good provider. Neither one of them, of course, could foresee that during the Depression years Gerald would turn out to be a more reliable and steadier provider for his family than many of the more educated, more cultured, and wealthier men about whom Irene dreamed in the abstract might have been.

Still, Irene swallowed her reticence, followed through with the wedding ceremony, and a little less than a year and a half later Jonathan arrived, followed fourteen months later by Joseph. As the Roaring Twenties took hold and America giddily celebrated for nearly a decade, Irene occasionally felt herself uncomfortably swallowed up by her two—and later three and even later four and five— children. Irene would read about and see pictures of "Flapper Girls" drinking in Speakeasies, smoking, doing the Charleston, and even reveling in previously unthinkable debauchery. Irene loved her children, and she had grown to love her husband, but in unguarded moments the thought came to her: she was missing out; missing out on *life itself*.

And that, Irene realized, was her quandary with what to do about Charlene. On one hand, in a reincarnation of her own mother, she saw Larry Moncheck as a sturdy, reasonable husband for her daughter: several years hence, of course. Charlene's life—Charlene Moncheck's life— would, someday after the war, mirror Irene's own. Larry would pick up some sort of trade, maybe even open up his own little shop or business or otherwise work in one of

Pittsburgh's factories or steel mills. They would have three or four or maybe even five children, and twenty or twenty-five years hence, Charlene would repeat the cycle all over with her oldest daughter, Irene watching from the sidelines if she was still alive.

(All of this assumed that Larry survived the war as Gerald Coleman had survived an earlier one, Irene realized, but she *forbid* that thought from entering her mind because it would, of course, force her to wonder whether her own sons would come home alive.)

But if all that happened, what would Charlene be missing out on? The same things that had passed over and skipped by Irene's life? When 1966 came around and Charlene was the same age as Irene was now, would she look back on the previous twenty years, fighting back twinges of regret at what she had missed because of the choice she had made, to marry that particular man at that particular time?

As Irene stood in Gimbel's sporting goods department, waiting for Joseph's and Thomas' baseball gloves to be wrapped (she could save almost a dollar on each glove compared to Horne's, where Gerald had had the inspiration for those gifts, and Irene was certain to make sure she purchased the exact models that Gerald had written down for her), the scenes playing in front of Irene's eyes suddenly shifted from her own past and Charlene's future to the present, four miles or so away from where she was now. She now saw the inside of her own house, the now-ancient wallpaper in all the downstairs rooms and hers and Gerald's bedroom yellowed from years of cigarette smoke... and just age, as if the wallpaper itself had grown weary from years of struggle. Now the scene shifted to one of those elegant homes she had dreamed about as a girl, Henry Frick's *Clayton* on the other side of Pittsburgh, how she had imagined herself marrying into the Frick family and entertaining the Mellons in *her* home...

My God, what am I doing? Irene Coleman actually shook her head in short, quick notions to force those scenes from her mind and bring her back to the present, to *reality*. Why now, as she was so desperately trying to create a wonderful Christmas for her family—her *real* husband and children, not some imaginary husband and children who never existed—were these emotions swirling around and inside her? How could she possibly let any regrets about the path her life had taken and the man she had married seep into her thoughts like some kind of cancer?

Irene Coleman's life was what it was. The question of the moment, she insisted to herself, was what her daughter's life would be... and, the critical decision Irene needed to make, how much of a role she would have herself in trying to fashion the shape of Charlene's life.

Joseph Coleman, slumped on the living room floor, his back propped against the faded and worn reddish sofa, was bored. He wouldn't have rather been in school, of course, but on this second vacation day away from school, he wished there were something more exciting to do than just sit around the Coleman family room, absentmindedly twirling the radio's dial between the same music and war news that his father was listening to a short distance away in his shop. Joseph had even asked his father if he could help out at the shop that day but his father had evasively answered that he had a lot to do today and tomorrow, maybe Friday after Christmas. Joseph insightfully assumed that his banishment from his father's shop had something to do with Gerald hand-making a Christmas gift for at least one family member, so he didn't press the issue and instead lounged around the house throughout the morning and into the afternoon.

The previous night's uneasiness about the war, catalyzed by the department store window displays, had vanished, and Joseph daydreamed about being with the Marine defenders of Wake Island or the Army troops in the Philippines, single-handedly fighting off the attacking Japs and being celebrated across America as "the new Sergeant York." He saw himself with the Flying Tigers, shooting down five or six Zeroes each time he went up in his P-40B Tomahawk and becoming America's greatest all-time ace, surpassing the tally of the same Eddie Rickenbacker in whose biplane his father had once flown.

His daydreams were interrupted by the front door opening as Jonathan entered, shaking off the cold, his miraculously snow-free boots clasped in his left hand. Like the rest of the Coleman children, Jonathan knew better than to bring a single snowflake through that front door at the penalty of his mother's wrath, so he had spent a good minute violently shaking and brushing every possible flake of snow from the water-stained, beaten leather shells and soles.

"Hey, Joey," Jonathan called to his brother. Only when his parents were present did Jonathan adhere to his mother's edict that all children would be called by their exact Christian names, little Ruthie the only exception. Jonathan usually used "Joey," occasionally the simple and terse "Joe," but almost never "Joseph" without the presence of at least one of their parents.

"Is it warming up at all?" Joseph asked him.

"What, you too lazy to get off your butt and walk outside to see for yourself?" Jonathan chided his brother good-naturedly.

Joseph just shrugged, his boredom picked up loud and clear by his brother.

"Want to go throw the football outside?" Jonathan asked, and Joseph suddenly perked up at the invitation.

"Sure!" he replied eagerly, and using his right arm began to rise.

"Let me get something to eat first," Jonathan replied, shedding his overcoat onto the coat rack by the front door.

Joseph got up and dutifully followed his brother into the kitchen, plopping into his customary seat while Jonathan rummaged through icebox and cabinet, finally deciding on a couple of peanut butter and jelly sandwiches. As he made the sandwiches, the rest of the Coleman children materialized in the kitchen, one by one; apparently everyone was bored, Jonathan thought with amusement, thinking knowingly that if any one had just finished ten hours of work, boredom in the midst of a cozily warm living room would be rather welcome.

Soon everyone began helping themselves to after-lunch-before-dinner snacks, Joseph and Thomas following their older brother's lead with peanut butter and jelly sandwiches, Charlene settling for a cup of tea and a couple of saltines after she got a glass of milk and a chocolate chip cookie for Ruth. Conversation soon turned to the subject of Christmas gifts, and cognizant of Ruthie's presence, everyone speculated on what Santa would be bringing them the following night after they were all asleep, snuggled in their beds.

The thought suddenly occurred to Ruth.

"How does Santa know what to bring you if you don't sit on his lap and tell him?" she asked all of them together, though her gaze was fixed on Jonathan; the oldest, the wisest, the almost-adult.

Jonathan, thinking quickly, was ready with an answer.

"We wrote letters to Santa telling him what we wanted, just like you did," he replied, reminding Ruthie of two weeks earlier when, for the first time, she personally and painstakingly printed her very own letter to Santa instead of dictating her list of coveted presents to her mother, who transcribed her daughter's wishes onto paper, as in previous years.

Thomas jumped in.

"But Charlene wants to go sit on Santa's lap," he said mischievously, not only getting Charlene back for the same remark about Thomas the night before but throwing in a bit of sexual innuendo, "don't you, Charlene?"

Charlene's eyes narrowed but before she could offer a retort, it was Joseph's turn.

"Only if Larry Moncheck got a job as Santa's helper, then she'd sit on his lap all day…"

Jonathan cleared his throat in that same "Attention! All conversation *will* cease right now!" manner that his mother had mastered long ago and through which Irene kept kitchen table bickering to an absolute minimum; an inherited trait, apparently. He shot a warning glance at Joseph, and Joseph picked up on Jonathan's message: don't talk about "getting a job as Santa's helper" in front of Ruth; Santa's helpers *were* Santa's helpers, not hired help.

Jonathan's commanding throat-clearing also cut off Charlene's rebuttal, for which she was glad. Saying *anything* about Larry now could be treading into dangerous territory, and she didn't want to discuss him at all with her blabbermouth brothers or even her sister, who wouldn't know enough not to innocently relate incriminating information to their mother.

Having gulped down his sandwiches, Jonathan nodded to Joseph.

"You ready, Joey?" he said, getting up from his seat.

"Where are you going?" Thomas asked.

"Outside," Joseph answered his younger brother, "we're going to throw the football around for a while."

"Can I come, too?" Thomas asked, his voice and eyes pleading.

Jonathan hesitated; he actually wanted to have a little bit of time alone with Joseph to talk something over. But catching the eager look in Thomas' eyes, he relented.

"Sure, Tommy," he nodded, and Thomas' eyes lit up with glee as if Santa himself had just dropped through the chimney with a sackful of presents for all five of them, and also news that the war was suddenly over as quickly as it had begun.

Jonathan felt a bit sorry for Thomas. The first seven years of his own life had coincided with much of the Roaring Twenties, and while the Coleman family was never extremely prosperous in those days (Irene Coleman was doing her best to force those same unwelcome thoughts from her mind at that very same moment), the general post-war climate during the Twenties was comfortable and peaceful. Even after the stock market crash things didn't immediately change much for the Coleman family until the Great Depression really took hold in 1931 and 1932, which meant that Jonathan still had a nickel to go to the Saturday afternoon movies or to buy candy or bubble gum baseball cards or small toys when he wanted.

Thomas, however, had been born in 1927, and by the time he reached his fifth birthday—the age at which Jonathan had first begun to explore the world outside the Coleman home—the Depression was in full swing, and life for *everyone*, even a five-year old like Thomas, was forever changed. A nickel for a Saturday afternoon movie? Maybe once every month or two, certainly not every week. Candy and baseball cards? Only on special occasions, like Thomas' birthday (also in October, 2 days after Jonathan's) and Easter. The new picture comic books? Only if Thomas could find a discarded one behind the school yard.

Thomas had been pressed into after-school service along with his brothers in his father's shoe repair shop when he turned seven in 1933, running errands for his father to take repaired shoes or boots to their owners' homes and to pick up payment, so Gerald could keep working in his shop and not lose valuable time making personal deliveries to his customers. Gerald would pay Thomas two or three cents from the proceeds of each of the deliveries, but caution the boy not to fritter away the money on treats or indulgences, that "a penny saved is a penny earned."

Thomas' childhood had been different, much more difficult than his own or even Joseph's, despite the relative closeness of their ages. And now, just as the Depression was finally giving way after a decade, the war comes, meaning that Joseph's high school years would have the shadow of eventual and inevitable military time hanging over them. So if a half hour or so of throwing a football with his brothers could give him some distracting pleasure, Jonathan thought, why not? Joseph retrieved the football from his bedroom and the three of them donned their overcoats and boots by the front door, heading outside into the impossibly bright sunshine. Unlike the previous few days no snow was forecast for today, and despite the cold the sun blazed as brightly as in the middle of the hottest summer day.

"OK, Marine," Joseph said, lightly shoving Thomas between his shoulder blades, "forward, march!"

Walking out into the street, the three brothers took up positions so the sun wouldn't be directly glaring into anyone's eyes, an unwelcome distraction—particularly for Thomas and Joseph when their oldest brother zipped the football with such velocity on every throw. For the better part of an hour they threw the ball around, first in a three-way triangle much as the older two had done two days earlier with their cousin Marty, and then—watching out for the occasional motorcar, of course—they ran one-on-one plays, Jonathan mostly throwing to one of his brothers while the other defended. Occasionally Joseph or Thomas took a turn at quarterback, and by the time the sun was in the better part of its downward trajectory as the afternoon began dying, all three were sweating profusely beneath their coats despite the cold.

Thomas was the first to give in to the growing winter bite, suggesting hopefully that they might call it a day, but waiting for acknowledgment from either Jonathan or Joseph that indeed, the afternoon's "game" was now concluded.

"Yeah, Tommy," Joseph said, "I whipped your butt enough for the day." But before he could also turn towards the house he caught sight of Jonathan flicking out his left index finger towards Joseph in a "wait a minute" sign.

"We'll be in in a minute, Tommy," Jonathan said. Thomas looked hesitatingly back at them, but Jonathan nodded towards the house, saying,

"I just need to talk with Joey about something, it'll only take a minute."

Ordinarily Thomas' feelings would be at least a little bit hurt by being left out of whatever topic of conversation Jonathan had in mind, but after standing still for a few minutes every exposed part of his skin was becoming increasingly numb from the iciness, so he didn't object. After Thomas completed the shaking-off-the-snow ritual outside the front door and then disappeared inside the house, Jonathan turned to his brother.

"Joey, I want to talk to you about all of this dropping out of high school to enlist business you keep bringing up."

Joseph cocked his head.

"What do you mean?" he asked.

"How about just laying off of all of that, you know, not mentioning it around the house? Around Ma and Pa?"

"Why?" Joseph countered defensively.

"Come on," Jonathan's voice suddenly commanding, like an officer giving orders to one of his reluctant troops, "don't tell me you can't see how upset Ma gets every time you bring it up. Pa too, even though he hides it better and usually doesn't say anything."

Jonathan suddenly flipped the football underhanded to Joseph, who reflexively reached out his hands to catch the toss.

"Look," Jonathan continued, "I know you're just trying to be like everybody else, we're all going to get into this one way or another. But why rush it, and why keep talking about dropping out of school? Ma hears that and first, she worries that you'll get killed in the war, and then she worries that after you come back you'll be, what, twenty-one or twenty-two, depending on how long this thing lasts, right? You'll come back without your diploma, and you know how important that is to her."

Joseph started to object, but Jonathan cut him off.

"And to make it worse, Ma is so set on having this special Christmas for all of us despite the war, and before all the rationing starts, she wants everything to be just perfect, you know, nobody worrying about what's going on out there." Jonathan made a broad sweeping motion with his right arm, indicating "out there" meant all over Pittsburgh, the rest of the state and the country beyond the city, and even the rest of the world beyond that.

"Look," Jonathan went on, "I'm not telling you what to do; I haven't made up my mind myself, whether to enlist or wait until they draft me. I'm just telling you to shut up"—he said "shut up" in a friendly enough tone so his brother wouldn't take particular offense, but also shouldn't be mistaken about Jonathan's message—"about enlisting and especially about dropping out of school... especially now and until at least after New Year's. Talk it over with Pa then, talk it over with me, but mostly let Ma have her special Christmas without having to worry about you disappearing from home one day and showing up a couple days later wearing an Army uniform."

Joseph just shrugged, and then tossed the football back to Jonathan, almost a sign of yielding to his brother's request.

"Yeah, OK," Joseph said, "I guess I can do that."

An uncomfortable look suddenly came to Joseph's face.

"What do you think it's like?" Joseph hesitatingly asked his brother.

Neither one needed any amplification on "it;" "it" meant the Army or the Navy, boot camp, the overcrowded Liberty ship pitching in the waves all the way across the Atlantic or Pacific, the first time in combat. "It" meant all of that, and more.

"I don't know," Jonathan answered just as quietly, his commanding demeanor of only a moment before evaporating. He shook his head, and repeated himself:

"I don't know."

"From what Pa told us, it can't be too bad, right?" Joseph asked, just as a child just catching onto the truth about Santa Claus might ask his mother "There's really a Santa Claus, right?" but knowing deep down that his mother would tell him what he wanted to hear, not the truth.

But Jonathan, shrugging, did not have a mother's diplomacy.

"Remember, Pa was never in combat," he answered. "If we wind up doing something like he did, you know, supply sergeant or whatever, then maybe it won't be too bad. But if we wind up in the infantry or armor or artillery..."

Joseph cut him off.

"So maybe the Navy will be better," he proposed in the same wishful tones.

"I don't think so," Jonathan countered. "Look what happened to all the ships at Pearl Harbor, all the sailors who got killed. Then you got the U-boats sinking all those ships in the Atlantic, and we don't even have lots of troop transports going over yet; I think it will only get worse."

Joseph's mind appeared to be whirling, the chess player whose first two proposed moves were countered, now looking for yet another alternative.

"I think it's going to be luck of the draw," Jonathan continued. "Whether it's Navy or Army, or Air Corps or even the Marines, we might wind up in the middle of it or we might not; I don't think there's any way to tell."

He looked at his brother, Joseph's face oozing worry.

"But you know what?" Jonathan offered. "Even if we wind up in the infantry or whatever, I think the chances are pretty good we'll come through it OK. By the time we get into it things won't be like they are now, you know, with all those poor bastards in the Philippines and on Wake Island outnumbered by the Japs because they got caught by surprise and can't get any reinforcements in there. We'll probably be with an invasion force that will be so large that either the Japs or Germans will be so outnumbered we'll run right over them and go straight for Tokyo or Berlin, and the war will be over in a flash."

Joseph knew, and Jonathan knew that Joseph knew, that Jonathan's words were little more than wishful optimism. The truth was that neither one of them could possibly know what awaited them... so they could spend the weeks and months until "it" happened increasingly worried and fearful, or they could simply accept whatever fate they would soon be dealt and keep living their lives much as they had before December 7th.

It was Joseph who segued the conversation back from the brink by changing the subject.

"Why do you think Ma is making such a big deal about this Christmas?" he asked Jonathan. "I mean, it's only Ruthie that still believes in Santa Claus, and with everything that's going on..."

Jonathan interrupted.

"That's just it," he explained, "it's *because* of everything that's going on. I know, she seems to be making too big of a deal about it for all of us except Ruthie, but think about it; this is the last Christmas we'll all be together until after the war"—he left unspoken "if you and I make it through alive"—"and then after the war there will be Francine and whoever you marry, and maybe Charlene too..."

Joseph's head jerked towards his brother. Francine? Before he had a chance to say or ask anything, Jonathan's face broke into one of the widest grins Joseph had ever seen. In words eerily similar to those their sister had spoken to their cousin Lorraine two days earlier (though neither one knew this, of course), Jonathan said,

"You can't say anything to anybody, *especially* Ma and Pa, but tomorrow on Christmas Eve I'm going to ask Francine to marry me."

Joseph's eyes were wide; for a while he was speechless. True, Jonathan was no longer a high school kid, he was a man with a job, a man who got up at some unholy hour in the darkness every morning and went to work for ten hours down on the Strip District. Still, because Jonathan still slept in the same room he always had, Joseph's mind had refused to make the leap to the point where his brother would be that close to getting married and moving out. True, he had been going steady with Francine for two years now, but Francine was still "Jonathan's girlfriend," just as she had been in high school. His wife, though?

"I got a ring for her," Jonathan said, words spilling forth, thrilled to finally have someone to talk to about his fiancé-to-be. "I'm going to give it to her tomorrow afternoon when I go over there, that will be her Christmas present."

"When are you going to get married?" Joseph asked, still not believing what he was hearing.

Jonathan shrugged, flipping the football back to Joseph.

"I don't know," he answered, "I guess it depends on whether I enlist and when they send me to boot camp, or if I wait around to get drafted. I'd like to wait until April or May, you know how girls all want to get married in the spring, but if I enlist or get drafted earlier then I guess we'll get married before I ship out. I figure she'll be here, waiting for me to get back..."

His voice drifted out, the sentence unfinished.

"Wow," was all Joseph could muster as he absorbed all the news.

"Like I said," Jonathan warned, "don't say anything to Ma and Pa about this. I'm not going to say anything until after Christmas is over, I just hope that Francine's parents don't call here after she tells them, you know, the in-laws talking things over and all that."

"Wow," Joseph repeated as the sun accelerated its descent and the late December cold finally overtook both of them and they headed towards the house.

❀ ❀ ❀

Supper that evening was a surprisingly strained affair, but Gerald assumed that the uncharacteristic silence on Irene's part was due to having been even more on the run than usual all day long. She hadn't made it back home from downtown until after 5:00, loaded down with three shopping bags in each hand, slump-shouldered from the combined weight of all of the packages. Jonathan caught sight of his mother coming up the still snow-packed sidewalk before he could hear the clump of her steps on the wooden porch, and he nodded to Charlene to hustle Ruthie into the kitchen under the ruse of "helping" Charlene set the table. Jonathan quietly opened the front door and walked out to meet his mother, taking all six shopping bags from her in a single fluid motion.

"Ruthie is in the kitchen with Charlene," he said in a low voice, "I'll get these upstairs."

Irene only nodded, knowing that Jonathan knew enough to stash the shopping bags full of presents in the clothes closet of his parents' bedroom, not only out of Ruthie's sight but in a place where none of the other Coleman children would dare snoop and pry, even knowing where the presents were. Indeed, Jonathan felt so uneasy trespassing in his parents' room, even with his mother's "pass" to hide the presents, that he quickly plopped the packages into the closet, shut the closet door, and then also closed the bedroom door behind him.

In the meantime, Irene had headed into the kitchen, involuntarily shooting Charlene a peering, knowing glance as she fell right into the ritual of preparing supper as if she had been in the kitchen for the past hour. Charlene had already turned away from her mother towards Ruthie, however, and didn't notice her mother's look.

But Charlene had plenty of opportunity to catch that same look during supper, as did Gerald, who wondered what Charlene had done to earn such disproportional attention from her mother. Normally during any family meal Irene was the consummate mother-diplomat, dividing her time as equally as possible among whichever of her children were gathered around the table for that meal... traditionally all five of them, though with Jonathan working in mornings and afternoons and often out with Francine on Saturday evenings, the more common number in the past year was "four."

Tonight, however, conversation from Irene was sparse and almost every moment she wasn't looking at her own plate, her eyes were boring into Charlene, who wondered just what in the world her mother's problem was... not that she was going to ask, of course, she knew that the best approach was that if her mother didn't bring up one infraction or shortcoming or another, she certainly wasn't going to do so.

Nowhere in Charlene's thoughts was the possibility that her mother had learned the news of her secret engagement; she assumed that her mother was simply tired from having trekked all over the city all day, and

Charlene had missed out on some chore or another that her mother had immediately noticed upon her return home. If Irene followed true to pattern, she would simply take care of the skipped dusting or sweeping or window cleaning or whatever it was by herself, yet put extra emphasis on her directive the next time she asked Charlene to do that task.

Later that night, though, just after 9:30, the phone rang and Joseph jumped up from listening to *Fibber McGee and Molly* to thoughtfully grab the phone off of the cradle before the loud bell could wake Jonathan or Ruthie, who had both gone to bed a half hour earlier. When Jonathan began heading to bed at 8:30, 9:00, or some other early hour because of his early morning workday, Joseph and Thomas had both teased him that all of a sudden he was going to bed at the same time as Ruthie, sometimes even earlier than the youngest of them all. Jonathan had just grumbled to both of them, "wait until you have to get up in the middle of night to go to work, see if you want to stay up late then," and eventually his brothers tired of the running joke.

"It's for you," Joseph turned back to Charlene, holding the phone to her.

"Is it Larry?" Charlene asked as she used her right arm to push off of the floor right in front of the radio where she had been lounging, the radio's volume turned down so the sound didn't echo through the thin walls into either Jonathan's or Ruthie's room. Gerald was plopped into his easy chair, reading the afternoon *Pittsburgh Sun-Telegraph*, and Irene was doing some final tidying-up in the kitchen.

"No, it's Lorraine," Joseph answered and immediately the cold sweat of panicky fear enveloped Charlene's body. She hesitated for a brief instant before abruptly grabbing the phone from Joseph.

"Hello?" Charlene said hesitatingly.

"Your mother knows about you and Larry," came the warning in her cousin's contrite-filled voice.

4—Wednesday, December 24, 1941

"Crispmas Eve!" was Ruth Coleman's first thought of the morning as sleep faded and the initial wisps of sunlight filtered through the opaque, icy film that had formed overnight on both the inside and outside surfaces of the bedroom window above her small bed. Later tonight, right after Ruthie went to bed and fell asleep, Santa would come down their chimney bringing *her* presents with him!

A week earlier, Ruthie, ever the schemer, offered this proposal to her mother: how about if, right after awakening on Christmas Eve morning as she had just done, she fell immediately back to sleep? She would now be asleep after having been awake, and it would be Christmas Eve; wouldn't Santa bring her presents right then and put them under the tree downstairs, on Christmas Eve morning?

Irene tried patiently to explain "Eve" as the root of the word "evening," meaning after the clock reached a certain time, but Ruthie couldn't quite follow the logic until Irene finally and firmly told Ruthie that Santa followed a regular schedule every year that didn't start until that night, long after dark had fallen... and there could be no exceptions, even for little girls who tried to trick Santa by falling back asleep on Christmas Eve morning.

Resigned to the agonizing day-long anticipation that awaited her, Ruthie pushed her thick layer of bedcovers away and felt the first blast of the chilled bedroom air begin to penetrate through her flannel pajamas. The exposed skin of her face and hands had already become acclimated to the cold, and the rest of her body would soon also warm up. She sat up and dangled her footie-covered feet against the side of her bed and then slid her body down the side edge of the bed until she reached the floor. Ruthie walked across her room through the open bedroom door (hers was still the only one that Irene prohibited being closed at night, her reasoning being that she could more easily hear if her youngest suddenly began choking or was overtaken by a coughing fit, or any one of a hundred other motherly worries).

Being the first one awake Ruthie didn't have to wait for the bathroom to become available, and after a quick visit she plodded her way down the stairs, adhering to her mother's rule to hold the handrail all the way down so the fabric bottom of her footie pajamas didn't suddenly send her sliding down the stairs on her backside. Her mother was already in the kitchen, mixing batter for this morning's breakfast main course—hotcakes—and hearing Ruthie slide into the room, she turned around and forced a smile on her face, saying "Good morning, Ruthie." Ruthie, glancing back over her shoulder at the Christmas tree in the dining room just to check and see if maybe Santa's schedule got mixed up and he came to the Coleman house one night early, didn't notice that her mother's voice wasn't quite as cheerful as usual when greeting her daughter.

"Would you like a glass of milk before breakfast?" Irene asked, a little bit closer to normal tones this time.

"Uh-huh," Ruthie nodded and waited expectedly as her mother retrieved a half-sized glass from the closet and reached for the milk bottle that was sitting next to the sink. Pouring the glass half-full and handing it to Ruthie, she said,

"Be careful, don't bang your tooth on the glass; I don't think the tooth fairy can come the same day that Santa does."

Suddenly sensitive to her loose front tooth that was ready to fall out any day now, Ruthie thought that an extra nickel from the tooth fairy would certainly be welcome in addition to the presents that Santa would be bringing, but she could certainly wait an extra day or two for that nickel; there was no sense in losing a tooth if the tooth fairy couldn't come anyway and she'd wind up cheated out of the nickel.

Thomas was the next to arrive in the kitchen, followed a few seconds later by Joseph. Irene greeted them in much the same way that she had greeted Ruthie, a bit more tersely than usual, but neither took notice. It wasn't until Charlene showed up ten minutes later and was welcomed by her mother with a reprise of the previous night's glare-and-sparing-talk communication that Joseph shot his brother a "I wonder what's up?" glance when their mother turned her back to them for a second.

The front door opened and Gerald came in, shaking off the cold after shoveling away the inch or so of snow that had fallen overnight. He greeted his children a touch more warmly than his wife had, first kissing Ruthie on the top of her head, and then patting each of the others on their shoulders, a gruff yet affectionate "g'mornin'" for each.

Irene had begun plopping batter into the two greased stovetop cooking pans, carefully watching over the hotcakes as they cooked and flipping each one the second she felt it was ready to be turned over. Gerald and the boys could each be expected to polish off a good half-dozen of Irene's generously sized cakes, Charlene three or maybe even four, and Ruthie one. Irene could fit two hotcakes into each pan, which meant that each of the children would be served one from the first batch, with Gerald waiting for the second batch for his first helping. Irene would, as she always did when hotcakes were on the menu, keep the batter flowing into the cooking pans and the hotcakes delivered to the table as efficiently as any war plant assembly line until all at the table had their fill, at which point Irene would finally prepare several hotcakes for herself.

The butter plate and bottle of maple syrup made its way around the table, rarely resting on the wooden surface for more than thirty seconds before someone asked that they be passed to top Irene's latest delivery to a breakfast plate. The morning conversation flowed in step with the butter and syrup, mostly a final speculation about what Santa would be bringing with him that evening and questions from Ruthie about exactly what route he would be taking through their Polish Hill neighborhood, if they'd be getting their presents before their cousins Marty and Lorraine did.

At the mention of Lorraine's name Charlene involuntarily stiffened and looked up from her plate towards her mother, who in turn looked back over her left shoulder at the table, directly at Charlene. Both Irene and Charlene had roughly the same thought, and wondered if the other did as well: how much longer would this little cat-and-mouse game go on?

The winter sky once again threatened snow as Gerald rounded the corner, heading towards his shop in a brisk pace to try and counter the icy morning air. The forecast called for two or three inches later that night, a Christmas Eve present for Pittsburghers if the snowflakes came gently tumbling from the sky as so many hoped. Gerald's plan was to finish up his work backlog by 3:00 that afternoon, 4:00 at the latest, so he could head home in time for supper before the family headed off to St. Michael's for Christmas Eve Mass.

He unlocked the shop's door and after shedding his overcoat—no shaking-off-snow-outside ritual as at home for Gerald, the snow from his boots and coat and hat would simply melt onto the worn pine floor planks and then evaporate into nothingness—and after surveying the boots and shoes on his "to do" shelf he set right to work. No radio this morning; no war news or Home Front news, he wanted to get going right away so he could finish on schedule. As he retrieved the tools of his trade from his worn satchel and set them side by side on his workbench, Gerald's mind briefly wandered ahead to the following Monday and for perhaps the hundredth time during the past few days wondered what awaited him in his new foreman's job in the factory up on Mt. Washington. He stared longingly at the curved leather sewing needle and the forty-year old cutting shears that he kept frighteningly sharpened, and felt a sudden sadness that in his new job he would no longer work with those and other tools in his own hands for eight, ten, even twelve hours some days. Instead he would be overseeing others who would be doing very much as he had done all his life, and he wondered what it would be like, watching others create and perhaps repair (Did they also do repairs at the plant or just make new shoes and boots, Gerald suddenly wondered, realizing that he didn't know the answer) rather than doing the creating and repairing himself, tools in hand. He once again vowed to himself that no matter how many hours he worked at the plant each day, no matter how tired he was, that he'd still make the time to do the one or two side jobs each day as planned so the void wouldn't be quite so severe.

Just before ten o'clock that morning Gerald heard the doorknob turn and the door groan open, shooting a blast of cold air into the shop. He looked back over his shoulder and saw the face of Karol Rzepecki peering at Gerald, shutting the door behind him. Gerald suddenly felt his stomach drop, almost exactly the same feeling as if he were riding the Jackrabbit roller coaster with one of the boys out at Kennywood Park.

Neither man said anything for a moment; neither man seemed to know what to say. Finally, Karol Rzepecki broke the silence.

"I wanted to pick up my dress shoes," he said hesitatingly, not adding—but Gerald knew anyway— "before the funeral next week."

Gerald simply nodded, and looked up at his "finished" shelf and located the pair of freshly shined, newly resoled black shoes that he had dropped off with Gerald more than a week earlier, two days after he had received the news that his 24-year old son Paul, the oldest of his nine children, had been killed during the attacks on Pearl Harbor and the other bases in Hawaii. Like several other boys from Polish Hill and other Pittsburgh neighborhoods, Paul Rzepecki had joined the Army in the mid-1930s mostly for a place to sleep and three meals a day after he wasn't able to catch on with a WPA crew. Karol Rzepecki had been out of steady work for several years and his son's thinking was that by joining the Army his father had one less mouth to feed in a house that was still packed with his eight younger brothers and sisters.

Paul had been thrilled when, in early 1941, he was transferred to Hickam Field in Hawaii, given the opportunity to actually live in an exotic location that he never thought he'd actually have the chance to see. He wrote his parents frequently, often sending home photographs of himself against a backdrop of ancient Hawaiian monuments or lush plants and flowers, telling them that he was able to save a few dollars each month and maybe he'd be able to buy them a pair of third-class tickets on a steamer so they could visit Hawaii someday while he was still there.

The telegram didn't arrive at the Rzepecki home until four days after the attack, but neither Karol nor his wife Margaret was surprised when the olive green Army car pulled up in front of their house and the somber-faced Lieutenant exited and began slowly walking up their sidewalk to the front door. Both had *felt* that their son had been killed in the attack, and though neither one could actually say those words to the other, they both had begun preparing for the worst.

Paul's body was scheduled to arrive back in San Francisco Friday, and depending on the train schedules and weather along the tracks would most likely arrive in Pittsburgh the following Tuesday or Wednesday. The funeral service would be held two or three days later, right after a very somber New Year's, the entire neighborhood expected to pay their final respects to the first boy from Polish Hill to die in the war.

"How is Margaret holding up?" Gerald asked and Karol just shrugged.

"She has her bad days," he answered, "but she's strong, she keeps going. She has the others to take care of..."

His voice trailed off and the silence once again was awkward.

"How are *you* holding up?" Gerald asked, a highly uncharacteristic question from one stoic workman to another, each only one generation removed from their immigrant fathers, each always taking such care not to show too much emotion to their families or to anyone else.

Karol exhaled, a "so what can I do anyway but keep going?" sigh.

"I don't think it's really sunk in yet," he answered Gerald's question. "Probably not until we have him back and we bury him."

Gerald handed the shoes to Karol, who in turn handed Gerald two silver dollars. Gerald felt incredibly uncomfortable, taking money from a man whose son had just been killed, a man who could barely afford to pay to have his only pair of dress shoes repaired, and only because he would need to wear them to his son's funeral. Both men had known each other since they were boys; Karol was two years older than Gerald and in grammar school had even selected Gerald as a bullying target one year, regularly taunting Gerald and occasionally beating him up. As they outgrew this childishness the bullying stopped and the two became regular acquaintances, if not exactly the closest of friends. Karol had been a regular customer of Gerald's ever since Gerald took over his father's shop, almost as if Karol were trying to make up for his bad behavior as a youngster by giving his shoe repair business to the same boy-turned-man whom he used to torment.

But now Karol Rzepecki seemed a shell of his former self, not only far removed from the young bully he once had been but even the man he was only three weeks earlier. Gerald wondered how many other neighborhood fathers would walk through the doors of his shop over the next two years, three years, or however long the war lasted, having only recently received the terrible news that their sons had been killed in the war.

The transaction complete, Karol turned to leave.

"We'll all be there," Gerald told him, and Karol turned back and nodded his gratitude before heading back into the winter gray. Even after he shut the door behind him, Karol's sorrow stayed behind in the shop, enveloping Gerald in a mournful aura.

Right before Christmas, Gerald thought sadly; it's terrible enough to lose your son this way, no matter what time of year, but from now on Karol and Margaret and their other children would always associate Christmas as the season in which their son or brother had died so young.

The first Christmas of the war, Gerald suddenly thought. How many more wartime Christmases would there be, he wondered, and how many more Christmas season deaths would bring sorrow to families just like Karol's?

Or maybe even his own family; he couldn't force that thought away, it would hang there, ever present, until that first Christmas *after* the war arrived, his sons home once again. Gerald turned his attention back to pulling the old soles from Joe Lepczyk's work boots, and then reached to turn on the radio's knob. There was no escaping war news in one form or another, he realized, so no sense in hiding from the world in his little shop tucked safely inside a Pittsburgh neighborhood. Might as well listen to some Christmas music, Gerald thought, even if the news from the war would violate the airwaves sooner or later.

It was a good thing that Gerald accepted the inevitable, because a half hour later came the news that the optimism from Monday morning's *Post-Gazette* headline about relief being on the way to Wake Island apparently had been nothing more than wishful thinking, maybe even just a mirage.

The United States Marine Corps had surrendered Wake Island to the Japanese yesterday.

The rest of the morning and the early part of the afternoon passed uneventfully at the Coleman household. Thomas and Joseph threw the football around in the street before lunch, Charlene kept to herself in her room avoiding her mother, and Ruthie watched the second hand on one clock or another in the house tick by with excruciating slowness. Jonathan came home from work at lunch time— Old Man Weisberg let his workers who weren't Jewish go home an hour or so earlier than usual since it was Christmas Eve—and it seemed to Irene that Jonathan was acting as if the weight of the world had suddenly come to rest on his shoulders. Still undecided about when and how to confront Charlene, Irene had no time to worry about any possible problems (most likely *imagined* problems) with Jonathan. When Jonathan announced at 4:20 that afternoon that he was leaving to go give Francine her Christmas present, Joseph gave him a conspiratorial in-the-know look and Irene gave him a stern warning that he was to be home by 5:45, no later, for supper before heading to St. Michael's. Jonathan promised that he would, at the same time thinking that he wouldn't be surprised if he was fifteen minutes or so late for dinner and he already began thinking of his alibi.

Charlene came down the stairs just as the door shut behind Jonathan, and Irene turned to her daughter and said,

"Jonathan is going to give Francine her Christmas present." Pause... pause... pause... "Did Larry give you *your* present yet?"

One point for Irene Coleman.

Charlene felt the fury begin to overtake her. Not only did her mother know her secret, she was toying with Charlene as well, trying to force Charlene to confess rather than confront her daughter with what she now knew. Well, two can play this game, Charlene thought.

"Not yet," she replied, her voice innocence personified. "I expect that he'll wait until Christmas Day to come over and bring me his *gift*"—Charlene put bite into the word—"or maybe he'll even wait until later, I'm not sure."

Charlene then added, wondering even as she said the words if she should be going this far (but she did anyway), "I'm sure he has something very special in mind for me."

The score was now tied: Irene and Charlene, one point each.

"I'm sure he does," Irene sniffed, and turned towards the kitchen.

For now, a time-out in this epic battle, the outcome still able to go either way.

❀ ❀ ❀

Francine Donner's house was no more than a ten-minute walk from Jonathan's own; he usually covered the distance in even less time but today he walked a bit more slowly, a bit more deliberately, trying to time his arrival for exactly 4:30 as he had agreed with Francine on the phone the day before. Everything had to be perfect this afternoon, from a precise on-time arrival to exactly the words he would use, the position he would take (kneeling in front of her, of course) when he asked her The Question.

Francine lived in a corner house and Jonathan arrived at the black iron gate with 25 seconds to spare, according to his quick glance at his watch. He pulled back the bar that served as the gate latch and pushed the gate forward, entered Her Domain, and turned back to make sure he relatched the gate behind him. The Donners' sidewalk was still snow-covered, Francine's mother obviously not as demanding of a snow-free walkway as his own mother was.

He shuffled forward carefully—the last thing he wanted to do now was go sprawling in front of Francine, who no doubt was peeking through the front window curtains as her beloved came to her—and took each of the three stairs up to the faded blue wooden-floored porch with equal caution. Cognizant of the snow that was no doubt still plastered to the soles of his boots, he trod just as carefully across the six feet or so of snow-free but still wet porch floor he had to cross before reaching the front door.

Jonathan took a deep breath, and then knocked on the front door with his gloved right hand, the knocking sound more muffled than if his knuckles had been bare in more moderate weather. A few seconds later, he heard the door being unlatched from inside and looked down at the doorknob as it turned, and then back up at Francine's face for the first time in almost a week and a half.

"Hi," he said, smiling, waiting to be invited inside.

"Hello, Jonathan," she replied, also smiling as she reached out to clasp his gloved right hand with her left one. "Come in, it's *freezing* out here!"

"OK," Jonathan said, pulling his hand back as he stomped the snow from his boots just as carefully as if he were home, then shedding his overcoat and shaking the snow from it, directed away from the open doorway. He peeled off his gloves and shoved them into his coat pockets and as free of snow as he was going to be, followed Francine inside.

"My parents are over at my Aunt Joan's," Francine said as Jonathan hung his overcoat on the hall coat stand that was positioned almost exactly by the front door as the one in his own home, "they took Joey and Charlene over there to see the Christmas tree." From the time they had begun dating Jonathan felt that it was more than coincidence that he and Francine each had a brother named Joseph and a sister named Charlene. Fate; it could only be fate, and as they had become more serious he occasionally chuckled to himself (but never saying anything to Francine, of course) thinking how confusing it would be someday for their children to have two Uncle Joes and two Aunt Charlenes, one from each side of the family.

"So we're all alone," Francine's eyes twinkled as she reached for Jonathan's hands, both of them this time, and pulled him towards her, leaning towards Jonathan at the same time. Jonathan's last remaining hesitancy from a week and a half of absence evaporated as their bodies and lips came together.

The kiss lasted longer and was far more intimate than any other "hello kiss" that Jonathan could ever recall between the two of them. Ordinarily the passion of opened mouths and touching tongues didn't surface until well into a date, in the back row at the movie house or somewhere else where they had enough privacy to make out. Never before, though, in Francine's house, Jonathan also realizing that this was the first time he had ever been there when neither of Francine's parents were present to stand guard over their daughter.

He felt Francine press ever more closely against him and he involuntarily leaned back slightly, embarrassed at his physical reaction to the intimacy right in the middle of her living room, in broad daylight (or what was left of it, the sun preparing to slither beneath the horizon behind the overcast winter sky). As he was shifting his lower body slightly backward he felt a touch of a smirk come to her lips even as they were still pressed against his, her tongue far more active than it had ever been before during one of their kisses.

He broke the kiss and opened his eyes just as Francine opened hers.

"So where's my Christmas gift?" she asked.

Jonathan nodded his head towards the door, towards the coat stand where his overcoat was.

"It's in my coat pocket over there," he replied.

"Ooooh, something small enough for your coat pocket," Francine cooed. "I'll bet it's jewelry, right? Earrings? A necklace?"

Jonathan just shrugged, suddenly uneasy at the seductive look in Francine's eyes, the seductive tone of her voice, her seductive behavior... all very much out of character for her. Not necessarily unwelcome, he thought, but certainly out of character.

"Wait here," Francine said, "I'll go get your present."

She turned towards the stairs, took two steps and then whirled and flung herself at Jonathan, locking lips with him again as she pressed herself tightly against him.

Where is this coming from? Jonathan wondered even as his tongue sought hers, suddenly uneasy. There was more here than just the conclusion of a week and a half's absence...

Francine broke away again, this time continuing towards the stairs and up to her room, returning with a compact book-sized giftwrapped package, the wrapping finished with thin strands of gold-colored ribbon and a blood-red bow.

"You go first," Francine said, nodding towards Jonathan's coat that he had indicated held his gift for Francine.

"Um, why don't you go first?" Jonathan suggested, thinking that after he gave Francine the ring and the accompanying marriage proposal, everything else would be anti-climactic. And he certainly didn't want to upstage the effort Francine had gone to to pick out and buy whatever it was she had gotten Jonathan; she should certainly go first.

"OK," Francine agreed. "Sit down," she gently nudged Jonathan so he plopped back onto the Donners' gold sofa, handing him the package as he came to a rest against the sofa back before sitting herself to his right and snuggling against him.

Jonathan gently pulled away the string and ran his index finger along the seam of the wrapping paper, assuming that Francine would appreciate his taking care to do as little damage to her giftwrapping job as possible rather than just tear the paper away as a savage might do. The paper now removed, he gently removed the top box with its gold "Kaufmann's" embossed lettering to reveal the off-white tissue paper surrounding a plaid scarf.

"I hope that you like it," Francine said hopefully.

"I do," Jonathan said, and indeed, it was a nice scarf. When he brought his only one out of the attic a month and a half earlier when the cold weather first hit Pittsburgh, he noticed how worn it had become. He expected that his mother might have a new scarf for him on her Christmas list, but he could certainly use an extra one if one would be placed for him under his Christmas tree later that night.

"Look underneath the scarf," Francine said, and Jonathan slid his hand beneath the scarf to find a smaller fist-sized gift-wrapped box.

"I got you something else," Francine added, her eyes carefully watching as Jonathan repeated his careful unwrapping ritual. He opened the smaller box to reveal a golden collar stick resting against a layer of royal blue padding, held in place by two small loops of string.

"Wow!" Jonathan said. "It's great!" He had never owned a collar stick before, and had often admired the occasional one he saw among the better dressed men Sunday mornings at St. Michael's. In fact, he could wear it tonight for Christmas Eve Mass and again tomorrow morning.

"I saw it and I thought it would look great on you," Francine said. "You can wear it to church"—obviously she was reading his mind, Jonathan thought—"and also when you take me out to a fancy restaurant with all that money you're making."

"Yeah," Jonathan said, suddenly seeing an image of himself squiring an elegantly dressed Francine to a fancy party at Webster Hall in Oakland, himself dressed in the finest pinstriped suit, a blood-red silk tie resting on top of Francine's collar stick. Suddenly the vision clouded: maybe after the war, he thought.

"Thank you," Jonathan said, leaning to his right to kiss Francine, who returned the kiss once again with an abundance of passion.

Again breaking the kiss, Jonathan suddenly felt the butterflies and a nauseous feeling as The Moment arrived. He got up from the sofa and crossed over to his coat and withdrew his own fist-sized giftwrapped package. He went back to the sofa, gently sat down in the same place he had just vacated—the butterflies were worse now, and Jonathan felt almost as if he were about to throw up—as he handed the package to Francine.

He had rehearsed the timing of what would happen next over and over in his mind. She would remove the giftwrapping but before she could open the jewelry box, Jonathan would reach over and take her hands—and the box—into his, and launch into his proposal, then *he* would open the box to show her the ring, hopefully timed perfectly with her "Yes" answer.

It all went wrong from the second he held the package out to her. The dancing seductiveness suddenly vanished from her eyes, the smile from her lips. She hesitatingly took the box from him, but held it in her hands, not removing the wrapping at all.

Jonathan's butterflies of nervousness yielded to a truly sick feeling. He felt his mind whirl, doing its best to prepare for the worst.

But he had no idea at all yet what "the worst" really meant.

Francine finally began to slowly, hesitatingly tear at the seam of the wrapping paper, her eyes locked onto the package, not daring to look up into Jonathan's. The wrapping paper removed, what she *knew* was a ring box right in front of her, Jonathan's hands reaching across to take hers...

Francine yanked her hands back away from his, not wanting him to touch her. She leaned away from Jonathan, shifting her body to break all points of contact with him.

She flicked open the box lid, took a quick glance at the diamond, nodded, and shut the lid again, tears suddenly glistening in her eyes. Jonathan had assumed that probably he'd see tears when she looked at the diamond, but he instantly knew that these weren't... well, they weren't *those* kind of tears, tears of joy.

Francine sat there, clasping and staring at the jewelry box, and then finally looked up at Jonathan.

"Why did you do this?" she asked, her voice cracking.

Jonathan didn't know how to answer, because he wasn't quite sure exactly what her question meant.

"Now," she added, then put her entire question together and asked him again, now sobbing.

"Why did you do this now?"

All Jonathan could think to do was answer her question with another question in return.

"What do you mean?" he asked, now completely and thoroughly confused.

"Now," she repeated in a single, sobbing word, as if that should clear everything up for Jonathan.

"I don't understand," Jonathan said. "What's wrong? Did you want me to wait until after Christmas to ask you?"

"I didn't want you to ask me at all!" Francine yelled at him. "Not until enough time had passed since..."

She didn't finish the sentence, but Jonathan had a sinking feeling that he knew the unspoken words.

"Since what?" he asked, his eyes narrowing.

Francine didn't answer him right away. She got up from the sofa, took a couple of steps to her right and then forward—moving further and further away from Jonathan with every step—and then opened the jewelry box again, this time gazing at the ring for an agonizingly long five or six seconds before shutting the box... forever.

"Something happened with Donnie," she said, looking again not at Jonathan but at the jewelry box. And then, as if realizing that combining the words she had just said with the gift Jonathan had attempted to give her was almost an abomination, she crossed to the other side of Jonathan and set the ring box on the end table; she couldn't bear it in her grasp any longer.

"I didn't plan for it to happen," she continued, still looking away from Jonathan, "it just did. We went to a movie and then he took me to a nightclub and..."

Jonathan's butterflies were long gone, but the nausea was front and center, along with the feeling that his heart had climbed up his windpipe and was now lodged in his throat, making every breath an excruciating effort.

"And what?" he asked quickly, even though he didn't want to know the answer... or maybe he did, his mind was such a blur that if asked his name this very moment he would struggle for the correct response.

Francine didn't answer.

"And what?" Jonathan repeated, anger creeping into his voice.

"I don't want to say," she replied after an uncomfortable pause.

"Why not? You brought it up!" Jonathan was getting angry now. Here, he had assumed—no, he had taken Francine's word—that her date with Donnie was a simple "saying goodbye to a friend going off to war" event, a passing moment of little consequence. But now here she was, telling him that he had been a fool to take her at her word.

"Don't yell at me," Francine said quietly, her sobbing subsiding. "I didn't mean to hurt you, it just happened."

"*What* just happened?" Jonathan demanded again.

Francine just sighed and began sobbing again, but she choked off the sob; she was done crying, done doing her penance.

"*It* happened, alright?"

❀ ❀ ❀

She had sworn to herself, even while Donnie was still inside her, grunting, that Jonathan would never learn about this, at least from her. As long as Donnie left for boot camp on schedule a week later and didn't run into Jonathan—or if he did, and he kept his mouth shut like a gentleman—Jonathan never needed to know.

Until her second whiskey sour at the Crawford Grille, the nightclub Francine had long hoped she'd go to one day, she had no intentions of Donnie getting anything from her other than a peck on the cheek when he finally dropped her off at home later that night. But the drinks went to her head and she was just as intoxicated by the nightclub's ambiance: the club's band playing the Dorsey's music and also Benny Goodman's; the gay celebrating crowd of businessmen and their wives; more than a few uniformed soldiers and sailors home in Pittsburgh for Christmas leave from Fort Dix or Pensacola or Wright Field or wherever they were stationed, some with wives or dates and others cruising around the club looking for companionship for the duration of their leave... or perhaps just for the evening.

Francine had never felt so much like an adult as she did that night, and Donnie Yablonski did his best to make her feel that this indeed was a magical evening.... for both of them. Lightheaded, now sipping her third drink, Francine couldn't keep a wicked smile from her lips and her eyes when Donnie sidled up to her, put his left arm authoritatively around the lowest possible part of her waist, his pinkie and ring finger drooped downward, actually pressing intimately against the top of her rear end, and pulled her towards him.

"Let's get out of here," he offered, his voice indicating that he was confident in what her answer would be.

"I don't know," Francine replied hesitatingly, but making no attempt to pull back away from him. In her mind's alcohol-induced fog confusing scenes were playing in which Donnie and Jonathan were intertwined, almost as if they were a single fused person. Jonathan, her current boyfriend of two years, with whom increasing degrees of intimacy were becoming more frequent, even though they hadn't "done it" yet; and Donnie, who had preceded Jonathan in her life and her heart and who had been all but out of her life and her mind for so long now, but was here with her at this very moment, offering Francine the "opportunity" to take yet one more step towards full-fledged womanhood...

The rest of the evening was mostly a blur to Francine, at least in terms of the actual conversation and the exact timing and sequence of events. She recalled with perfect clarity, of course, how the evening had ended up: Donnie Yablonski taking her virginity in an elegantly furnished room at the William Penn hotel. She could remember much of what he had told her, how he was going off to war in a few short days and how he might not come back, and how he still loved Francine even though they had been apart for two years and how he wanted to remember her in a "special way." But had he begun cajoling Francine while they were still at the Crawford Grille, or was it after they were already kissing frantically in the Olds' back seat before he suggested adjourning to a hotel? Francine couldn't recall, but she did remember countering Donnie's "going off to war" declaration by correcting him, noting that he was actually going off to boot camp, and might never actually go off to war.

It didn't matter, though; she knew he was only giving her a line, and if Francine was honest with herself, Donnie's feeble reasoning and pleading wasn't even the reason she wound up in the hotel room with Donnie, hoping that he would hurry and finish so he could get her home before 1:00. Her parents would be furious enough, and despite her near-drunkenness and the weight of Donnie's body bearing down on her she was already concocting an alibi for her parents: Donnie's Olds breaking down, Donnie shivering in the cold while he fixed the engine or changed the tires or whatever her story would be.

No, it was finally getting the opportunity to act as a grownup for one night that had weakened her resistance, and even as Donnie was undressing her and putting his fingers where Jonathan's—or any other boy's or man's— had never been, and even as he was putting whatever that was over his you-know-what so she wouldn't get pregnant, and as he was rolling on top of her and she prepared herself for whatever it would be that she would feel at the instant "it" happened... even as all of this was occurring, and afterwards as well, she wished that it were Jonathan, not Donnie, that was doing all of this with her.

❀ ❀ ❀

"Tell me this: what was all that when I came in, you know, the kissing and everything?" Jonathan's angry question brought her mind back from reliving the previous Friday night to the present.

Francine knew the answer to his question, but she didn't know exactly the right words to use. Even as Donnie was driving her home, so obviously very pleased with his conquest, Francine was wondering how she could repair the terrible damage she had done to her relationship with Jonathan. The plan had already begun formulating itself while she was still in the passenger seat of Donnie's Olds: just act like none of this had actually happened. It was so simple; Jonathan never needed to know (assuming, again, that Donnie didn't spill the secret), and the next time she saw Jonathan she'd kiss him so very passionately and make him feel so very special...

She'd buy him an extra-special Christmas present, not just the scarf she had already bought but something else as well, maybe a piece of men's jewelry that Jonathan could wear when he dressed up in a suit and took her to the Crawford Grille or the Villa Madrid or some other nightclub.

Time would pass and the memory—and the feeling—of what had happened barely an hour earlier would fade, and she could go on with Jonathan as if this whole episode had never happened. For all Jonathan would know, she had gone to a movie with Donnie and then to the Crawford for a couple of drinks; it had been a pleasant enough evening with an old friend, and nothing more. And when Donnie came back to Pittsburgh someday he hopefully wouldn't say anything, a gentleman wouldn't...

Or maybe Donnie would be killed in the war, and the secret would die with him. Even as this thought was still occurring to her Francine felt the shame of this sudden "solution" to her predicament, no matter how involuntary it was or how she immediately dismissed it. Wishing that

Donnie would die on some battlefield or be in a plane that was shot down over Europe or some ocean, only so her guilty secret would die with him? My God, is this what she was already turning into barely an hour after becoming a woman, if that's what her first time actually meant?

Francine had avoided Jonathan's calls on Monday. She had been at home each time he had called and her parents had done her dirty work for her, deflecting Jonathan's attempts to contact her. She didn't feel quite ready to put her charade into action, not just yet; she needed another day to steel her mind and her will, to thoroughly convince herself that Friday night actually hadn't happened, it had all been a dream... yes, that's it, simply a dream that faded with the reality of daylight.

And so when Jonathan called on Tuesday morning— only yesterday, though now it seemed to Francine months or even years ago as her entire scheme was falling apart— she was ready for him. Then she had greeted him when he came over minutes earlier as she had planned, not just with an abundance of affection but also, in away, transferring the intimacy she had briefly extended to Donnie to Jonathan. Jonathan could take her to a hotel room at the William Penn, sign in alone and then sneak her past the hotel detective up to the room, and also make love to Francine. And if he wondered about the apparent lack of any signs of Francine's virginity, she'd make up some kind of medical explanation; men didn't know much about these things anyway, Francine figured.

It could all work; it *would* all work, just as Francine had calculated.

But then, as soon as she realized what Jonathan's Christmas present was—not just the ring, but the offer of marriage—the entire plan fell apart. She *couldn't* go through with it, not at that moment. If only he hadn't asked her to marry him until a month later, maybe two months, until she had had time to purge her guilt for what she had allowed Donnie to do only days earlier. But because Jonathan had unknowingly not waited until anywhere near enough time had passed, his choked-off proposal had caused a flood of shame for what Francine had intended, and she couldn't go through with it. She wanted to marry Jonathan and to become his wife, but she couldn't be this unfair to him; the timing was all wrong.

Francine tried her best to put her reasoning into words, and in the middle of her jumbled, confusing explanation she had a sudden flash that Jonathan would tell her that all was forgiven, that he loved her anyway and that if they let a little time pass they really could pick up as if nothing at all had happened with Donnie.

Jonathan wasn't thinking anything of the sort.

"So let me get this straight," he said, trying his best to keep his voice as level as possible, "if I hadn't asked you to marry me now, if I had come over with a sweater or a necklace or whatever as a Christmas present, you would have taken it and we'd go out this Saturday night and then next week on New Year's Eve, and things would have just gone on?"

Francine started to answer but he rolled right over her words.

"And then, if, say, in March or April before I shipped out I asked you to marry me then, you would have probably said 'yes' even though you had..."—he couldn't bring himself to say "sex with Donnie" or "slept with Donnie" or something even more explicit and vulgar—"you know, you would still have married me?"

"Uh-huh," Francine said contritely.

"I can't believe it!" Jonathan shouted, abandoning his attempt to keep his anger at bay. "You would have done that to me, treated me that way, after you... after you..."

He couldn't finish the sentence. Instead, he pushed himself up from the sofa, reached for the jewelry box sitting on the end table, and stomped over to the coat rack.

"Jonathan, wait," Francine said, but without much conviction in her voice. There actually wasn't much more that could be said, that should be said. She had made her confession, Jonathan had received it, and that was that. Maybe she had been foolish to think that after what she had allowed Donnie to do there could possibly have been any future with Jonathan, that that future had died the moment she walked into that hotel room with Donnie... or if not then, then certainly when she lay naked in bed with Donnie and he rolled over on top of her and she gave herself to him.

Jonathan ignored her words, slid into his overcoat, and didn't look back as he opened the front door and left the Donner house just as the last of the day's sun disappeared below the horizon.

As the door closed behind Jonathan (he had the decency not to slam it shut, much as he would have liked to), Francine looked over to the sofa and saw the opened box containing the scarf and collar stick, the package that

Jonathan had left behind almost as a symbol that everything between the two of them was now concluded.

At 5:45 sharp, Irene Coleman was mildly annoyed that Jonathan hadn't come home yet from Francine's. By 6:00, barely ten minutes before the family was to sit down for Christmas Eve supper, she was *very* annoyed. And at 6:15—she allowed an extra five minutes past the scheduled starting time for supper to give Jonathan a bit of extra time—she was now not only incredibly annoyed, she was also a bit worried. He had only been a few blocks away, certainly close enough to exchange presents with Francine and make it home during the course of almost two hours. Most likely they had slipped away somewhere to do some necking, Irene thought to herself, her fury barely in check; Jonathan might be nineteen years old but if he had promised his mother he'd be home in time for dinner and not only broke that promise but still wasn't home a half hour later... well God help him given the mood she was in because of what she had learned about Charlene. Christmas season or not, wartime or not, her children would *not* behave this discourteously to her; it just simply wouldn't be tolerated.

She finally called the family to the table and supper was a hushed affair, everyone—even Gerald—afraid that even the most innocent and unrelated comment would unleash Irene's rage. Charlene, however, was thankful for this unexpected turn of events, and hoped that Jonathan didn't show up for another few hours, and maybe even missed Christmas Eve Mass, to deflect Irene's attention from her.

And so Charlene's Christmas Eve wish came true.

❀ ❀ ❀

Jonathan wandered directionlessly, oblivious to the frigid night air. At first he shuffled around Polish Hill, but suddenly the surroundings felt suffocating, as if imbued with—no, make that poisoned by—Francine's nearby presence, her very existence. He had to put some distance between himself and her, and he began walking towards Oakland, more than two miles away. The streets and sidewalks were mostly deserted, most of Pittsburgh sitting down at this very moment to supper with their families. Only the faintest slivers of house lights filtered through the blackout curtains into the night for Jonathan and the few others out and about to see. After another hour had passed people would begin appearing again as the Catholics began walking through the blackness to the churches for Christmas Eve Mass. Some others might choose to drive, but the neighborhood air raid wardens had spread the word that driving that night was highly discouraged, though not absolutely banned so those who lived too far away from their churches to walk could still attend Mass. The reason: wild rumors of a planned massive Christmas Eve bombing run by the Luftwaffe along the east coast and perhaps also eastern steel towns like Pittsburgh and Cleveland, the attack plan supposedly spilled by a Nazi spy captured somewhere in New Jersey.

Yesterday, and even earlier this very day, he was a happy young man despite the specter of war hanging over him. No matter what Uncle Sam (not to mention the Nazis or the Japs) had in store for him, he'd at least have a brief period of blissful happiness with the girl he loved. But now, even that had been taken away from him... no, not actually taken away, more like turned away, as if held out in front of him and then cruelly yanked out of his reach forever before he could touch even a sliver of happiness.

So what now? The shock of Francine's revelation beginning to wear off, Jonathan—ever the pragmatic one, always trying to think one step ahead—was at a total loss to figure out what this all meant to him. He found himself beginning to think along the same lines as Francine's failed plan. Suppose he hadn't taken the engagement ring with him as a Christmas present; suppose he *had* waited until another couple months had passed. At this very moment he would be blissfully ignorant of what had happened between Donnie and Francine, but since Francine apparently wanted to put that behind her and had no intentions of breaking up with Jonathan, would ignorance be so bad?

But he had done it, there was no turning back; now what, Jonathan wondered as he kept walking and walking and walking.

Christmas Eve Mass at St. Michael's was scheduled to begin at 7:15, and because of the Colemans' late start at supper they had to hustle to make it to the church before services began.

"I guess Jonathan will just have to meet us at church," Irene said without much conviction in her voice as they all began donning their winter outerwear, obviously sensing that something was wrong. Still, there was no point sitting around the house, Jonathan would know that the family would have headed to St. Michael's by this time.

All the while Joseph was particularly quiet, he alone knowing the full story of Jonathan's Christmas gift for Francine. For a brief instant he thought of telling his mother not to worry, that it was for a *good* reason—a *really, really good* reason—that Jonathan was late, that her son was at this very moment engaged. But he knew that Jonathan would be furious with him if he betrayed his brother's confidence and besides, the reason that Jonathan hadn't shown up was probably because they had the house alone and he and Francine were getting into it hot and heavy... maybe even going all the way. And there was no way that Joseph could tell *that* to his mother, that was for sure.

Because of their later-than-usual arrival at St. Michael's the Coleman family wound up sitting much further back in the church than they usually did, which served to displease Irene even more. They found an empty stretch of space along one of the benches, a block large enough to seat all six of them, seven when—or if—Jonathan showed up. They slid into their seats and left a single space in the middle of them all reserved for Jonathan. Surrounding the empty space: Charlene to the left, Irene to the right, the space between them symbolic of the uneasy, widening distance between mother and daughter.

From the time they all took their seats until the priest began Mass, and during the entire service, every member of the Coleman family (even Ruthie when she was standing up and able to see over the bench back and through the bodies in front of her) scanned the backs of the heads in front of them trying to catch a glimpse of Jonathan under the assumption that he had been running late leaving Francine's and had headed directly to St. Michael's. But despite a couple of false alarms nobody was able to locate Jonathan, and both Gerald and Irene slowly came to the conclusion that their oldest son wasn't in St. Michael's at all.

So where was he?

The service concluded at 8:30, and the crowd began filing out of the church, heading home to whatever Christmas Eve rituals each family observed: singing carols, drinking eggnog, or perhaps opening a single present that night. As Irene walked past the last row of seats she almost collided with Sally Donner, walking just ahead of her husband and her three children, including Francine. Sally Donner cast a hard-eyed glance at Irene and then towards Gerald, and then back to Irene, but didn't say anything at all.

Irene broke the suddenly uncomfortable silence.

"Hello, Sally," she said.

"Hello," came the icy reply.

Irene looked back at Francine who was looking away, praying for the exiting crowd to stop dawdling and HURRY UP, FOR GOD'S SAKE so she could get away from Jonathan's family.

"Jonathan didn't come home for supper and we didn't see him here," Irene said matter-of-factly, deciding on the direct route: enough games for today.

"We haven't seen him," Sally sniffed. "We came home from my sister Joan's house and found Francine crying."

She scanned all of the Colemans lined up behind Irene, and then looked back at Irene.

"I don't know what he did to make Francine cry," Sally Donner said accusingly. "She wouldn't tell us," she continued, nodding towards Francine, "but I think it's a terrible thing to do on Christmas Eve."

Irene immediately went on the offensive; nobody, especially someone she didn't particularly care for like Sally Donner, would cast dispersions on her son.

"If they had a fight then I'm sure they'll work it out," Irene said through gritted teeth. "But there's two sides to every story, Sally, including I'm sure this one."

Not wanting to escalate things any further on Christmas Eve, Irene broke off the attack.

"Merry Christmas, Sally," she simply said before leading her family away. They all filed past the Donners, who were still waiting for the congestion on their side of the church aisle to clear, and as Joseph passed Francine he turned his head towards her. Francine had turned to watch them but sensing a mixture of insight and puzzlement in the way Joseph was looking at her, she again looked away, refusing to turn her head until she was certain enough time had passed for Joseph to have moved on.

Irene had hoped that by the time they arrived home Jonathan would be waiting for them. He wasn't, but a burly, sour-looking police beat cop was.

Gerald Coleman felt his heart jump into his throat as the policeman whom he didn't recognize—he wasn't one of the regular Polish Hill cops, all of whom Gerald knew well from them making their rounds through the neighborhood—saw the approaching parents and children and rose from the wooden rocking chair on the Coleman's front porch in which he was sitting, waiting for them to return from church.

"You Gerald Coleman?" he growled in Gerald's direction, certain of the answer but determined to immediately seize the upper hand in this confrontation by speaking first.

Gerald nodded and was barely able to whisper a quiet "Yes."

"I got your son down at the station in Oakland. You gotta come down and get him out."

"What did he do?" Irene Coleman demanded. Her son Jonathan in trouble with the law? Impossible!

The cop's tone softened a bit—but just a touch—as he answered Irene's question.

"He got into a fight with the sergeant down at the Army recruiting office in Oakland," the cop replied.

Both Gerald and Irene Coleman had the identical thought simultaneously: recruiting office? What in the world was Jonathan doing down at the Army recruiting office in Oakland, especially on Christmas Eve when he should have been enjoying dinner and attending Christmas Eve Mass with his family?

"You take the children inside," Gerald said, turning to Irene. "I'll go see what this is all about."

Irene turned towards the four children, all of whom were staring wide-eyed at the cop standing on their front porch, not fully understanding what they had heard in the adults' exchange. Jonathan in trouble? Jonathan getting into a fight? Jonathan at the Army recruiting office?

Irene hustled them all into the front yard and past the policeman, single-file, as the cop was heading in the opposite direction, down the stairs and out to the sidewalk where Gerald Coleman still was. Gerald looked across the street and for the first time noticed the police squad car sitting in front of the Shalanskys' house, and assumed—correctly—that for the first time in his life, he would be taking a ride in a police car.

Until Gerald returned—hopefully with Jonathan in tow, and hopefully with some explanation for this incredible turn of events—she did her best to keep things as normal as possible around the house. Irene boiled water and made hot cocoa for the children and brewed coffee for herself, making enough so there would be some for Gerald when he returned home. The Colemans had never been ones for household singing—Christmas carols or otherwise—which was fortunate, given the half-hearted nature in which *Hark the Herald Angels Sing* and *Jingle Bells* would have come out of their mouths, everyone worrying about Jonathan.

Ruthie was sent off to bed at 9:30, a little bit later than usual because of Christmas Eve. The bottom of the Christmas tree was still void of presents but as soon as Ruthie had fallen asleep, her sister and brothers went to their rooms and retrieved the presents they had bought for each other, bringing them downstairs and arranging them around the tree's base. Irene would wait until the others headed to their beds before she would bring the rest of the gifts from her bedroom closet.

Charlene was the next to retire, followed shortly afterwards by Thomas. Irene was puttering around the kitchen, trying to keep her mind off of her worries about Jonathan that had taken front and center from those about Charlene, when Joseph walked in.

"Ma, can I talk to you?" Joseph barely got the words out of his mouth.

Irene looked his way, the look itself giving Joseph permission to continue.

"It's about Jonathan," Joseph continued.

"What?" Irene asked sharply, demandingly.

"I think I know what happened, you know, why he didn't show up for dinner or church, and why he might have gotten into trouble."

"Well why didn't you say anything before?" his mother growled through clenched teeth.

"He made me promise not to say anything," Joseph just about whined his response, growing angry at Jonathan for putting him in this spot.

"Well?"

Joseph took a deep breath.

"Remember when he went to give Francine her Christmas present?"

The look on Irene's face was pure "Get on with it!" so Joseph got right to the point.

"He was going to ask her to marry him," he said, adding "her Christmas present was an engagement ring."

"Jesus," Irene said involuntarily, violating one of her own rules.

"I guess she must have said no," Joseph reasoned, "I mean, if her mother said that she had been crying and everything. I just thought that when he didn't come home it was because she had said yes and they were..."

Joseph quickly shifted gears; he didn't dare head down *that* road.

"... you know, talking about the wedding and he lost track of time or something."

Irene just stood there, silently, stunned by the news. If Joseph was right and Francine had turned down his proposal—and all indications were indeed, that was what had happened—then that certainly explained why he had apparently gone off the deep end. There were still some things left to be explained, of course: why Jonathan had wound up at the Army recruiting office and, more importantly, why he had gotten into a fight, but Irene figured that the answers would be forthcoming soon enough.

Finally, Irene rested her left hand on Joseph's right shoulder, giving it an "it will be all right, really" squeeze.

"Go to bed now, I'll wait up for your father and Jonathan."

Joseph didn't need to be told twice; he wanted to be as far away from that conversation as possible, and he just about flew up the stairs.

The cop explained enough on the short drive to the Oakland police station that Gerald knew what had happened, if not why. Shortly after 7:00 Jonathan had arrived at the Army recruiting station in Oakland. The office had shut down at 5:00 because it was Christmas Eve, but a recruiting sergeant was still there, finishing up some paperwork before heading out in a probably futile search for an open bar to grab a beer or two. The door had been unlocked, and Jonathan walked in, shivering from walking in the cold for more than two hours.

"I wanna sign up," Jonathan had slurred as if he had been drunk; in fact, his speech was that way because his face was nearly totally numb. The sergeant wasn't sure why a drunk-sounding kid was showing up on Christmas Eve two hours after the station had closed to enlist in the Army, but he dismissively told Jonathan they were closed and to come back the day after Christmas since the station would be closed the next day.

Jonathan was in no mood for yet another "no" answer this day—the one several hours earlier from Francine had been devastating enough—and he insisted that he be allowed to enlist, right there and then.

"Look, buddy," the sergeant had said, exasperated that he had to put up with this when he was trying to close up shop for the night, "I told ya, come back on Friday when we reopen and I'll sign you up then."

Before Jonathan had a chance to argue, the sergeant—in response to the way Jonathan's voice sounded—looked up at the nineteen-year old with the red eyes and red nose, and said,

"And make sure you're sober when you come back then, we don't sign up no drunks."

For some reason, the sergeant's unsubstantiated charge flipped a switch in Jonathan, and he charged towards the desk, reaching across to grab the sergeant by his shirt front, but instead only grabbed a handful of the sergeant's tie. The recruiter hadn't expected Jonathan's attack—after all, this was a Pittsburgh recruiting station on Christmas Eve, not some Pacific island where he was surrounded by Japs—but he recovered quickly enough to shove Jonathan away, saying,

"Hey buddy! I don't want no trouble here, just go home and sleep it off."

Jonathan attacked again, and this time the sergeant easily sidestepped Jonathan's clumsy lunge across the desk and reached to grab the back of Jonathan's neck, slamming his head and upper torso against the desk and holding him down, trying to give Jonathan a chance to cool off. If Jonathan had let up at that moment the sergeant would have released his grip, helped Jonathan up, and maybe offered him a pointer or two on close order combat before ushering him out the door. Instead, Jonathan struggled and almost broke free, causing the soldier to have to shift positions and hold Jonathan down even more forcefully.

Just then, an Oakland beat cop strolled by the front of the former candy store that was now the recruiting station, looked inside, and saw the sergeant engaged in apparent hand-to-hand combat with someone. The cop's first thought was that some Nazi spy had snuck in and was trying to... well, do *something*, the cop couldn't quite envision in that split second what damage a Nazi spy might want to cause in a Pittsburgh recruiting station on Christmas Eve, but no matter, something was going on inside.

The cop rushed in the unlocked door, reaching for his nightstick as he did, and came very close to giving Jonathan Coleman a preemptive clubbing over his head before the sergeant saw the latest turn of events in this strange Christmas Eve drama and yelled "No no no no!" to the cop, not wanting to see this idiotic kid get clubbed on his head.

Still pinning Jonathan to the desk, the recruiting sergeant quickly explained to the cop what had happened, and then he released his grip on Jonathan, figuring that if the kid went on the attack once more, this time the policeman could smack him with his nightstick; the kid would deserve that for being so stupid.

Jonathan, though, seeing that he was outnumbered and taking the cop's appearance as a warning that he had better get himself under control, slowly got up from the desk, looked in the direction of the recruiting sergeant, and then began walking towards the door, ready to slink away. The cop, however, wasn't having any of that, and assuming that at the very least Jonathan Coleman was guilty of public drunkenness, he growled threateningly at the boy, nightstick still in hand, "Uh-uh; yer comin' wid me."

❀ ❀ ❀

Getting his son released from the lockup was surprisingly easy for Gerald, though he had no frame of reference with which to compare this evening's procedures.

"We ain't gonna charge him with anythin'," the desk sergeant told him. "He wasn't drunk even though he sure sounded that way, and he didn't break anythin' up down at the recruitin' station. And even though he started the fight, that recruitin' sergeant don't wanna press charges."

The desk sergeant glared at Gerald, condemning the older man with his look, a look that said "So this is how you raise your boy? To start brawls on Christmas Eve?" Gerald felt a surge of anger but held his tongue; this wasn't his neighborhood but he knew it didn't pay to get on the bad side of cops. All kinds of things might start happening if he mouthed off back to a policeman, no matter how abrupt the cop was.

Within minutes Jonathan had appeared, staring at the floor, not daring to catch his father's eye. Gerald signed a paper thrust in front of him signifying that he now had custody of his son, and the two Colemans walked out of the police station to wait for a streetcar to take them back home to Polish Hill.

Jonathan didn't offer an explanation and—for the moment—Gerald didn't demand one. But both of them knew that as soon as they got home, the interrogation would begin then.

❀ ❀ ❀

"Into the kitchen," Gerald ordered before they even had shed their outer clothing at the doorway, arriving home a bit after 11:30. The streetcars were running on a reduced schedule since it was Christmas Eve, and Gerald and Jonathan had to wait almost half an hour in the iciness after leaving the police station, still no words exchanged between the two of them at all, until one came by the corner of Fifth and Craig.

Jonathan finished removing his coat and boots, saw his mother standing in the doorway leading to the kitchen, and sighed. He hadn't yet decided how much he was going to tell his father and mother about his absence this evening, why he had snapped... all of it. Maybe he'd do his best to hold out... only name, rank and serial number, just like a solder captured by the Japs or Germans was supposed to give, but nothing more.

He marched past his mother into the kitchen and plopped himself down into his regular chair at the table, then looked up towards both of his parents with a "Well, get on with it! Give me your best shot!" look. Gerald and Irene likewise took their regular seats, and a fraction of a second after settling in his chair, Gerald locked eyes with his son and demanded:

"I'm waiting."

Jonathan didn't reply. Irene was in no mood for evasiveness or hesitation; it was late, she still had presents to settle under the tree.

"He asked Francine to marry him and she said no," she said to her husband.

Jonathan shot her a look that conveyed the message: "How could you possibly know that!?" His first thought was that they had run into Francine and her family at St. Michael's that evening and either Francine had told Gerald and Irene or—more likely—she had told her parents and one of them, Mrs. Donner probably, had in turn told Gerald and Irene. Still, that didn't quite ring true to Jonathan. Her parents would no doubt have badgered Francine to learn why she had turned down Jonathan's proposal. Neither one of them was particularly fond of him, but to have a daughter turn down an offer of marriage from her steady boyfriend... well, her parents, even if they were secretly (or not so secretly) glad she had done so would demand to know exactly why. And he couldn't quite see Francine contritely informing her parents that their daughter was no longer a virgin, courtesy of one night in a hotel with Donnie Yablonski.

Then, Jonathan heard the creak of a door swinging upstairs, and it hit him: Joey! He felt the rage rise again. He had told his brother not to say anything. Even though the night had turned out nothing like what Jonathan had planned, his brother was still bound by that promise of secrecy. And he had not only broken that promise, he had spilled his guts to their mother! Telling their father would have been bad enough...

Jonathan's thoughts were broken by his father's voice.

"She said she wouldn't marry you, so you go down to the Army recruiting station in Oakland and start a fight with a sergeant?" The look on Gerald Coleman's face finished the thought without the need for words: What kind of idiotic kid did I raise? Why would you do something so incredibly stupid?

"I went down to sign up," Jonathan answered, determined to end this inquisition as quickly as possible. "The sergeant told me to come back on Friday, I got mad, and I guess things got out of hand."

"You 'guess things got out of hand?'" Gerald mocked his son's explanation. "Why would you start a fight with him just cause he did the smart thing and didn't let you enlist on the spot? He probably saw that you were upset about something and figured that you needed time to cool off."

Jonathan wanted to tell his father that that wasn't it at all. It was the sergeant's dismissive way of speaking to Jonathan, as if he couldn't be bothered dealing with someone so insignificant as the nineteen-year old standing in front of him earlier that evening. After what had happened at Francine's, the thought of being trivialized yet again had simply caused him to snap.

Instead, all Jonathan could manage was a muttered "I wasn't thinking clearly," at which point Irene Coleman picked up the questioning.

"What happened with Francine?" she demanded.

"She said 'no,'" Jonathan replied through clenched teeth. "You already know that; there isn't anything more to say."

"Yes there is," his mother countered. "Just saying that she wouldn't marry you wouldn't cause you to walk for hours in the cold down to Oakland and then all of a sudden want to enlist in the Army, whether or not you got into a fight. *Something* happened, and I want to know what it was!"

Jonathan shot a look in his father's direction that clearly communicated what he felt: I really don't want to talk about it but if I have to, I'd rather talk to you than Ma. His father, sensing his son's silent plea, started to gently tell his wife to let the boy be, that he'd handle things from here.

Suddenly it hit Gerald: he still had to retrieve Ruthie's bicycle that he had assembled earlier in the day from his shop, where he had kept it out of sight.

"I have to go get Ruthie's bicycle," he told Irene. "Jonathan can come with me, I'll talk to him there."

Irene almost told her husband that he hadn't done much of a job getting anything out of the boy on the way home from the police station, that she had learned more from a brief conversation with Joseph and when it came to extracting information from the five Coleman children, Gerald was a rank amateur when compared to his wife. Still, she held her tongue; no sense in starting an argument with Gerald this close to midnight, with sleep still probably two hours or more away for Gerald, Jonathan, and herself.

"Fine," she said. "I'll put the other presents under the tree and then you can put Ruthie's bicycle there when you come back."

"Go upstairs and wash up and then come with me to the shop," Gerald ordered his son. Jonathan just shrugged. By now exhaustion was catching up with him, but maybe it would be best to just confess the whole story to his father, who could then decide what to tell—and what not to tell— Irene Coleman about why Francine and he wouldn't be getting married, after all.

Jonathan headed up the steps, towards the bathroom, and as he reached the upper hallway landing he heard a door creak. He looked over and saw Joseph peeking out from the crack. Seeing that his older brother was alone, Joseph made a "pssst!" sound. Jonathan's eyes narrowed as he changed direction and walked towards his brother's room, heading inside as Joseph opened the door just wide enough for Jonathan to fit through. As soon as Jonathan was within a foot of his brother his right arm shot forward, as if stiff-arming a would-be tackler on the football field, and caught his brother squarely in the middle of his chest with his own open palm.

Stumbling backwards, Joseph let out an involuntary "Ow!"

"I told you not to say anything," Jonathan snarled, "But you couldn't even wait a couple of hours to open your mouth!"

"It's cause you were missing and they were worried about you," Joseph bleated. "It was only after the cop came to the house and Pa went down to get you out."

His younger brother's eyes pleading for forgiveness, Jonathan let go of the impulse to shove Joseph again.

"What happened?" Joseph asked.

Aware that his father was waiting for him downstairs, Jonathan replied,

"I'll tell you tomorrow."

"Tell me now," Joseph pleaded.

For some reason, the thought of doing a "trial run" of his explanation for his brother before confiding in his father suddenly seemed like a good idea to Jonathan. In fact, he thought, why not just get right to the heart of the matter. He gave his brother a 45-second synopsis of the evening's events, working backwards from the police station to the Army recruiting office to Francine's house.

"I gave her the ring and asked her to marry me and she not only said she wouldn't, she told me it's because she went all the way with Donnie last Saturday."

Joseph's eyes widened. For a brief moment, no words could come to his mouth. Then he realized the question that he needed to ask.

"You gonna go down and get him?"

At first, Jonathan didn't understand his brother's question, but then the meaning sunk in, or at least he thought it did.

"You mean Donnie?"

"Uh-huh," Joseph nodded. "You're gonna go down and beat all hell out of him, right?"

That thought hadn't even occurred to Jonathan at any point during the evening's incredible turn of events. Here he was, all this time, focusing his anger on Francine and then trying to take his anger out on some Army sergeant who, Jonathan knew, could probably kill Jonathan with his bare hands if he really wanted to instead of just pinning him against a desk until a cop came to take him away.

Though for a fleeting second Jonathan felt tremendous satisfaction at a mental image of seeing himself beating Donnie Yablonski to within an inch of his life, he knew that doing so was not only a waste of time, it wouldn't change what had happened with Francine the previous Saturday. In her jumbled, rambling explanation she had tried to tell Jonathan that the entire time she had been thinking of him instead of Donnie, and made it seem that Donnie had gotten her drunk and taken advantage of her. But no matter whose "fault" it had been, just like Francine said, *it* happened, and it was now an unchangeable fact of history.

Jonathan just shook his head as he turned to leave his brother's room so he could wash up, go to his father's shop, and just get things over with.

"You're gonna go get him?" Joseph asked again, this time disbelief creeping into his tone. "You're not gonna let him get away with that, are you?"

"It doesn't matter," Jonathan said. "It's done now."

"I knew you were afraid," Joseph said.

"What did you say?" Jonathan had pivoted back to face his brother.

"I said that you're afraid," his brother retorted. "You're afraid to fight the Japs or the Germans, and you're even afraid to go fight Donnie Yablonski after he goes all the way with your girl."

Before Jonathan could even react, Joseph added, venomously,

"I'll bet that's why you went to the recruiting station as late as you did, because you knew they were closed and you wouldn't have to enlist, but it would look like you tried…"

Joseph never finished the sentence. Jonathan's right arm shot out again, this time a clenched fist instead of an open palm at the end; this time connecting squarely with his brother's nose instead of his chest.

Stunned at first by the force of the blow and the instant eruption of blood, Joseph staggered back a couple of steps and then went on the attack, much as Jonathan had earlier that evening in the recruiting office. He charged his brother, lowering his head as if he were making a football field tackle, and plowed into Jonathan, the force of the collision carrying them out into the hallway as they glanced off the edge of the door.

The noise they made as they landed in the hallway brought both Gerald and Irene Coleman flying up the stairs. Seeing their two oldest sons locked in a death's embrace and seeing the blood from Joseph's nose spreading across Jonathan's shirt, Irene Coleman's hand shot to her own mouth as if choking off some horrible scream while Gerald bounded towards his sons, grabbing one of them with each of his hands and lifting them off of the ground as easily as if they were two infants.

Before either parent could demand to know what *now* was going on, Joseph shot out an accusing finger pointed directly at his brother's face.

"He started it!"

Gerald looked over at Jonathan, expecting to hear his other son counter that it had actually been Joseph that had "started it"—much as had been the case every time he had broken up a fight between the two of them when they were younger—but Jonathan remained silent, a look on his face that seemed to Gerald to be filled with rage, perhaps even hatred.

"You"—Gerald looked at Joseph—"go into the bathroom and get a cold compress for your nose, and then get back out here."

He released Joseph who instantly complied with his father's order.

"And you"—he looked over at Jonathan, still in his grasp—"Just how many fights do you plan on getting into tonight?"

For a brief instant Jonathan felt like taking a swing at his father but that urge quickly subsided. This had certainly been a terrible evening, perhaps the worst one Jonathan had ever experienced—he could remember none worse—but he knew that hitting his father (or even attempting to) would be a suicidal act. Besides, his anger was quickly subsiding, as if this final clash with his brother had been just the thing he had needed to release the fury that had been building up all night and hadn't quite been fully dispelled during his brief tussle with the recruiting sergeant.

Joseph came back into the hallway, a white washcloth pressed against his nose; the white slowly giving way to a reddish-pink hue as his blood seeped into the cloth. His mother beckoned him towards her with a single crook of her finger, and he meekly complied. She gently pulled the washcloth away from her son's nose, poked about a bit, and nodded satisfactorily to herself.

"It's not too bad," she said to all of them, to Gerald in particular, "the bleeding is already slowing down. He'll have some swelling but he got hit on the fleshy part, I'm pretty sure nothing is broken."

"Both of you, change clothes and come with me," Gerald ordered, looking at Jonathan's blood-smeared shirt.

Jonathan and Joseph silently complied, emerging from their respective rooms three minutes later at the same instant, glaring at each other but not daring to say a word. Gerald marched them down the stairs, ordered them to don their boots and coats, and led them out the door just as the clock struck midnight and marked the arrival of Christmas Day, 1941.

5—Thursday, December 25, 1941

Ruthie slowly came awake to the sound of the voices floating in the hallway. She fought her body's desire to immediately drift back to sleep, forcing her eyes open to verify the night's blackness.

Santa! It had to be Santa in the house this very moment! And since it sounded like more than one person talking, he must have brought one of his helpers with him to the Coleman house, probably because he had so many presents to bring for all five of them, plus gifts for her parents as well.

Now fully awake, Ruthie slid out from under her covers and hopped to the floor. She would sneak down the stairs, as quietly as possible, to take a look at Santa in action! She crossed the room towards her open door but the instant she placed her foot outside her room she was intercepted by her mother crossing quickly from the top of the stairs to Ruthie's doorway.

"What do you think you're doing?" Irene Coleman asked tersely, almost angrily.

Ruthie's mind whirled. Surely her mother must know that Santa Claus was downstairs in their house this very instant. Wouldn't her mother also want to sneak down the stairs with Ruthie to catch a glimpse of him?

Or maybe her mother had already met Santa, had actually talked to him; that possibility occurred to Ruthie. After all, how could she possibly not know that Santa was downstairs? She might have already been downstairs herself!

Ruthie sucked in her bottom lip between her teeth, unsure of how she should reply to her mother. She pointed to the head of the stairs and started to utter the word "Santa" but the syllables choked in her throat. Maybe there was some rule little Ruthie didn't know that declared you couldn't utter Santa's name while he was in the house; sort of like her mother's rule about not saying Jesus' name outside of church unless someone was saying grace.

Sensing her daughter's thoughts, Irene Coleman looked sternly at Ruthie, lowered her voice, and quietly said,

"I think Santa is downstairs right now. You don't want him to know that you're up and have him take your presents back to the North Pole with him, do you?"

Ruthie quickly and urgently shook her head from side to side.

"You better get back in bed right away," Irene said, nodding her head to Ruthie's room behind the little girl. "If he doesn't see or hear you he won't know you're awake and he'll leave your presents under the tree."

Ruthie did an about-face worthy of the slickest drilling soldier and headed straight back to her bed, boosting herself quickly onto and then under her covers without the usual struggle caused by the mismatch between the distance from the floor to the top of the mattress and Ruthie's height (or lack thereof). Irene had followed closely behind her daughter and once she saw Ruthie tucked beneath the covers she leaned over and kissed the girl on her forehead and said,

"Even if you can't go back to sleep you should shut your eyes and keep them closed. This way if Santa comes up the stairs and peeks into your room he won't see you awake, he'll think you're still sleeping."

Ruthie complied immediately, and as Irene turned to leave the girl's room she turned back and said,

"I'm going to close your bedroom door for a little while so Santa can't look in, and then after I think he's gone I'll open it back up. But make sure you keep your eyes closed and don't make a sound, OK?"

Ruthie, prone in her bed and eyes clamped shut, nodded her wordless agreement. Irene walked through the doorway and shut the bedroom door behind her. Ruthie would be awake for another ten or fifteen minutes, she figured, out of the excitement of thinking that Santa Claus was in the very same house with her at that moment, but soon enough exhaustion would overtake excitement and she'd fall back asleep.

As Irene exited Ruthie's room, another upstairs bedroom door opened: this one Charlene's, the older girl also awakened by the voices and the sounds of the boys' brief but intense fight. Seeing her mother in the hallway Charlene started to close her door but then she caught her mother's eyes and froze.

Why not get everything out in the open, Irene thought to herself. Gerald can deal with the boys; I'll deal with Charlene. She crossed the few brief steps from Ruthie's doorway to Charlene's, looked her daughter in the eyes, and said,

"Come back into your bedroom; I want to talk to you."

Gerald marched his sons the few short blocks to his shop. They waited wordlessly while he removed his right glove and fished in his pocket for the key to the shop door, and when the door was unlocked he indicated with a flick of his head that they were to continue marching inside. Nothing had thus far been said by any of the three of them, much as had been the case on the way home from the Oakland police station after retrieving Jonathan.

Without even pausing to remove his coat, he turned to Jonathan and for the second time in less than an hour said,

"I'm waiting."

Jonathan just shrugged.

"I hit him," he nodded towards his brother, "and I'm sorry. I got angry…"

Gerald interrupted his son, shaking his head.

"No," he cut off Jonathan's tepid explanation. "From the beginning; I want the whole story."

Jonathan sighed and began to speak as he removed his coat (Joseph did likewise, and Gerald finally began to shed his own outerwear). He told his father about having bought the engagement ring Monday evening during the family's downtown shopping trip, and how he had planned for a while to ask Francine to marry him. He related how he had gone to Francine's house earlier this evening— yesterday evening, actually, he realized, now that it was past midnight, but there was no need to quibble little details—had asked her, and she had said no.

"Why?" Gerald probed as Jonathan started to tell how he had left her house and begun his walk to Oakland. Jonathan's eyes again tried to plead that this was a private matter, but since whatever it was had not only caused his son to be taken in by the police but also to attack his younger brother on Christmas Eve, any right to privacy had been forfeited.

Still, Jonathan couldn't bring himself to utter the horrible words, as if by saying them out loud to his father *he himself* would make what had happened real, forever and ever. Gerald looked over at his other son.

"You know what happened." A statement, not a question.

Joseph glanced at his brother, then back at his father. "Uh-huh."

"Tell me." A command, not a request.

Joseph again looked at his brother, wondering if he would be attacked again if he were the one who said what his brother didn't want to. At least Pa is here to break it up if we get into it again, he thought, and then he said:

"She went all the way with Donnie Yablonski when they went out last Saturday."

Gerald looked over at Jonathan, all the pieces of the puzzle suddenly tumbling into place even without the need for any further amplification by either of his sons. The girl had kept this secret from Jonathan, revealing it only when faced with his marriage proposal. He had been so caught by surprise that...

"And that's why you went down to Oakland to enlist? Because your girl wouldn't marry you and at the same time you found she had messed around with your friend Donnie?"

Jonathan shrugged; an acknowledgment.

"So what was the reason for the fight with the Army sergeant? And why the fight with your brother?"

Jonathan tried another shrug-for-an-answer response, but his father suddenly roared:

"Answer me!"

Stunned, Jonathan blurted out the only response he could think of:

"I don't know."

Hearing what he expected to hear, Gerald's voice softened a bit.

"That's right: you *don't* know. But you know what *I* know? That you lost your cool. Not once, but twice, within a few hours of each other. No, make that three times. First, she tells you she won't marry you, so you suddenly decide you're going to sign up for the Army; just like that. Then you get down to the recruiting station, the sergeant won't let you do it, and you start a fight with him; that's two. Then for whatever reason, you start a fight with your brother. That's three!"

Gerald looked over at Joseph, his look commanding his son to tell him the truth.

"What did you say to your brother that caused him to hit you in the nose?"

Hearing the word "nose" Joseph was suddenly cognizant of the eerie combination of numbness and pain, but at least the bleeding had stopped and he was fairly sure that his mother was right, his nose wasn't broken. Just another bloody nose, like the many he had had when he was younger; just that this was the first one in several years, and the first one at the receiving end of a punch from his older brother.

"I told him that he should go down and get Donnie."

Knowing that wasn't all of it, Gerald demanded:

"And?"

"I told him that he was afraid to fight Donnie"—he again looked over at Jonathan then back at his father—"and also afraid to fight the Japs and Germans."

Gerald looked in Jonathan's direction.

"And you heard your brother say this, and you punched him in the nose?"

Jonathan started to shrug, but then answered:

"Uh-huh."

Satisfied that he now had extracted the necessary pieces of information from his boys, he blew out a breath as he walked into the back of the shop to retrieve Ruthie's bicycle. He wheeled it into the front and leaned it up against the store's wall, then looked from one son to the other, back and forth several times, before speaking.

"I'm going to say this once, and this is for both of you, not just Jonathan. If you lose your cool and do something stupid like both of you did tonight"—Joseph started to protest at his inclusion in the "something stupid" category, but a withering look from his father shut down any complaint—"and you're over in the war instead of here, you're going to wind up getting killed. It's that simple."

He paused for a few seconds to let his words sink in, then continued.

"You"—he looked at Jonathan—"just because something happens that you didn't expect and it feels like the end of the world, you still have to shake it off and not go flying off the handle, not thinking about the consequences of what you're about to do. You start a fight with a recruiting sergeant you don't even know; what does that have to do with Francine? Or for that matter, just because she tells you she won't marry you and you find out about her and some other fellow, what does that have to do with you all of a sudden wanting to join the Army? You want to be some big hero and win all kinds of medals to show her how wrong she was to turn you down? Or is it that you want to die a big hero so she'll feel sorry that she said no?"

Gerald looked over at his other son.

"And you find out what happened to your brother and all you can do is try and get him to go beat up Donnie, and tell him he's afraid to fight? Is that how you're going to be when you get in the war? Are you going to disobey your sergeant's or your captain's orders to stay put because *you* decide it's time to attack? Or maybe you're going to be the kind of soldier who gets into all kinds of fights during training with the other guys but when you get over to the war you freeze up and hide at the bottom of your foxhole because you're terrified now that you're in a *real* war, not just a make-believe one."

He again looked from one son to the other.

"Let this night be a lesson, and be glad that it happened here and not over there. I want both you boys to come home safe from the war, and if you can't keep your cool then the chances are real good that you're going to get killed, or at least seriously wounded."

Gerald choked down a swallow.

"I know your mother would be devastated; she wants you both home safe."

Both boys knew he was also speaking for himself, but neither one was surprised that their father couldn't put that sentiment into words.

"Let's go home; it's late," Gerald said, reaching for the bicycle. Jonathan and Joseph started to put their coats on again as their father ordered:

"You two shake hands and put this behind you."

Jonathan, already contrite for his attack on his brother and feeling even more ashamed after the censure delivered by his father, stuck out his hand first. Joseph reached and clasped it, and both of Gerald Coleman's sons left the shop with their father, the unexpected strife between them left behind in the night air as the three of them walked home.

❀ ❀ ❀

"I understand you're engaged," Irene said flatly, deciding not to mince words or dance around the subject.

Since learning the previous night from her cousin Lorraine that her secret was no longer a secret, Charlene had rehearsed in her mind, over and over, how she would respond when her mother finally confronted her. I'm sixteen years old, not a baby, she'd retort, and besides, I'm engaged, not married; we might not get married for another year when I'll be seventeen.

Or, taking a somewhat more confrontational approach, Charlene would simply say something like: So what? It's my business, not yours, and there's nothing you can do about it because I love Larry and we *will* get married.

Still, when The Moment of confrontation actually arrived, Charlene found herself responding (and cursing herself for failing to take the defiant stand she had rehearsed),

"Um, he asked me the other night and I said yes."

Pause... pause... pause... Irene Coleman had a natural timing when it came to mother-child conversations with her children, especially mother-daughter talks. She never broke eye contact with Charlene, who finally yielded and looked down at her lap.

"I see," Irene continued in the same flat, disapproving voice. Another pause... pause... pause...

"And where is your engagement ring?" Irene added after (by her calculation) a tactical amount of tension-filled silence had passed.

Charlene felt a curious combination of embarrassment and anger overtake her.

"I don't have one," she answered her mother's question in clipped tones.

"No engagement ring?" Irene retorted, her voice taking on an almost mocking tone. "Your young man asks you to marry him, you say yes, and he doesn't give you an engagement ring?"

Charlene was becoming angrier now... but was she angry at her mother, at Larry, or maybe even at herself? Her mother was just that: a mother, *her* mother, someone who couldn't possibly be expected to understand the love in a young girl's heart and the giddy, grown-up feeling that Charlene felt from being engaged. After all, Charlene had planned on keeping this engagement a secret from her mother as long as possible; it was only because of her cousin's loose lips that she sat here, in the first hour of Christmas morning, being grilled by her mother.

Angry at Larry; Charlene had suppressed that sentiment ever since Lorraine had brought up the subject of the lack of a wedding ring on Sunday afternoon. That really was some nerve he had, Charlene found herself thinking throughout the week whenever she let her guard down and the absent token of his supposed love percolated into her consciousness. Against her will, sitting here in front of her disapproving mother, Charlene asked herself that same awful question once again: was she really engaged after all?

"I'm surprised," Irene continued, introducing a touch of sarcasm into her words. "I would have thought that if Larry loved you so much to ask you to marry him"—now Irene shifted abruptly to an accusing tone—"and whatever else he asked you to do, the least he could have done was given you a ring like a gentleman."

"Nothing like that happened," Charlene retorted quickly, almost too quickly, her mind struggling to keep the memories (and the sensation) of Larry's exploring touch at bay, as if recalling those thoughts at this very moment would cause them to somehow leak from her brain and be picked up and read by her all-knowing mother.

"I'm sure," Irene replied skeptically, and then shifted into yet another approach. She crossed over to the foot of Charlene's bed and sat down next to her daughter, leaving about two inches of space between their bodies, as if signifying there was still a significant chasm that needed to be bridged, that *might* be bridged, but it was too early to tell.

"Tell me what happened," Irene said gently, looking to her right over at Charlene.

Charlene shrugged (coincidentally, at that very moment, Jonathan was shrugging downstairs in response to a question from Gerald; it was as if the confusing adolescent pain felt by a brother were somehow aligning with that of his sister), and then told her mother the story, leaving out the parts about Larry kissing her, Larry unhooking her brassiere and his roving hands, and where his roving hands eventually wound up. She told her mother about Larry's impending enlistment, and how he had said he wanted to marry her before he shipped out.

Irene sat quietly, listening to her daughter's words, and filling in the blanks from a combination of her own memories and a mother's intuition. Chief in her mind right now (though unspoken to her daughter) was trying to discern if her daughter might be pregnant, or have reason to worry about being pregnant. Irene found it unfathomable that a sixteen-year old girl, one who was well brought up, could even have reason to worry (or, more accurately, to cause her mother to have reason to worry), but Irene remembered those fancy-free days of not so long ago, in the 1920s, when stories abounded of girls Charlene's age, or even younger, being quietly sent away from their homes in East Liberty or the Hill District to "visit" out-of-town relatives, returning two or three years later with a child in tow and, hopefully, a husband to keep up the charade of respectability.

The Depression years seemed to quell the fervor for girls Charlene's age to put themselves in a position to get into trouble, but the Depression was past, so was it possible that a new set of morals was setting in?

Irene listened to her daughter's words, read her emotions, and by the time Charlene finished her explanation Irene was convinced that despite Larry's most urgent attempts (she had no illusions about that), Charlene hadn't yielded to his tempting pleas and wasn't In Trouble.

Then Irene asked her daughter a rapid-fire series of questions that seemed puzzling to Charlene, but she'd remember her mother's exact words for many, many years to come.

"Do you want to marry him? Do you really love him? I don't mean do you want to marry him tonight or tomorrow or the next day, I mean do you love him enough to want to marry him at all?"

Caught so totally off guard by the barrage of questions, Charlene could only utter the truth:

"I don't know."

❀ ❀ ❀

Irene had shifted her body to her right, closing the gap between mother and daughter, and had placed her right hand gently over Charlene's hands that were clasped in her lap.

"When I was your age I knew that I would marry your father someday," Irene began telling her daughter. "Just like now, the war had just started, at least for us. Your father went into the Army and he felt the same way about me, that he wanted to marry me. He was even a year older than Larry is, he was nineteen then, and I was almost exactly your age to the day when he told me he would be leaving soon. We talked it over and decided to wait until he came back before we got married, and that's what happened. Even then he spent a couple months courting me again before asking me to marry him, and then we waited another year and a half until he had taken over the shop from Grandpa. By that time my mother felt much better about me getting married than she would have if your father and I had gotten married before he went over there."

It was all a lie. It was true enough that Irene's mother with her old-country ways wouldn't have hesitated to see her sixteen-year old daughter as a bride, and Gerald's mother had also been encouraging the match for several years. But at sixteen, Irene was still deeply in the throes of her sophisticated, wealthy—and imagined—lovers-to-be, one of whom would of course sweep her away from her humble roots into a new life of elegance and leisure. Alas, it never happened and Irene had succumbed to her destiny, but for purposes of this talk with her daughter, Irene had no compunction about creating her own revisionist version of The Truth Circa 1917.

"You waited for him the entire time he was gone?" Charlene asked; she had never heard this story from her mother before, but since she had never been told anything to the contrary, that the sixteen-year old Irene Walker bore very little resemblance to the mother she knew, Charlene had no reason to suspect that her mother's story was somewhat less than truthful.

"I did," Irene nodded, thinking to herself: Well, at least that part is true, sort of.

"I didn't know that," Charlene said.

"Even though it's been so many years, I still remember how I felt, and I know how you feel. You think that if Larry leaves before you two get married that he'll meet some English or French girl and marry her, or come back and move to Scranton or Youngstown or somewhere else and you'll have missed your chance because you'll have been here waiting for him and then if he comes back and doesn't marry you, you'll have to start all over with some other boy."

Irene looked over at her daughter.

"Am I right?" Irene said.

"I'm not sure," Charlene answered, and she wasn't. She kept coming back to her mother's question that had caused Charlene to blurt out the truth: she honestly didn't know if she wanted to marry Larry at all, and if she were honest with herself, she was glad he hadn't given her an engagement ring. If she had accepted a ring, Charlene thought, then she would be locked into marrying Larry, whether she did so before he shipped out after boot camp or if she did as her mother had apparently done with Charlene's father, waited for Larry to return from the war.

When she was with Larry she felt things that she had never felt before, but even though Charlene didn't know all that much about love and sex, other than the one very clinical, dispassionate talk from Irene Coleman three years earlier—plus what she learned from talks with Lorraine and others, not to mention her own dabblings—Charlene had a sneaking suspicion that the emotions she felt had more to do with matters of sex (or whatever it was called that they were doing, if "sex" actually only applied to going all the way) than any feelings of love. She felt that she was under Larry's spell when they were together, but when they were apart he was... he was...

She wasn't sure what Larry was, she admitted to herself. Take now: she hadn't seen him since Saturday night, he hadn't called her at all, but Charlene didn't feel any pangs of loneliness as if her heart were aching terribly from his absence. Was that love? Charlene knew there wasn't a definitive, authoritative answer, but in her mind the answer was "no."

A squeeze from her mother's hand on hers snapped Charlene out of her reflective mind-wandering.

"I'll bet Larry said that he wanted to marry you so he'll have someone back here and someone to come home to, right?"

Irene's words caused Charlene's jaw to drop slightly in astonishment.

"How did you know?"

"Because that's what your father said to me," Irene lied again, silently praying that when she died and was judged for all the sins of her lifetime, this terrible sin of repeatedly lying to her daughter on Christmas Day would be seen by Jesus or St. Peter or God Himself, whomever it would be that would pass judgment on Irene Walker Coleman's eternal soul, as a necessary evil to save her daughter from making what would likely be a mistake with one of the most significant choices of her life.

"He said that he wanted to know that I'd be home waiting for him and praying for his safety, but as we talked about it we realized that I'd still be doing exactly that, waiting and praying for him, even if we weren't married."

Charlene was unable any longer to fight off the yawn that had been percolating for the past ten minutes, and Irene gave up trying to suppress her own yawn. Both of them were exhausted; all that there was to be said had been said, even though nothing had been settled.

"Just promise me that you'll think very carefully about whatever it is that you want to do about Larry," Irene said. "Don't let him pressure you into getting married because he wants to if you don't think you're ready."

"OK," Charlene said, realizing that her mother was willing to let this clash end in a draw. No mother-to-daughter demands to forswear anything else to do with Larry Moncheck, no dramatic utterances of "that boy is not welcome in this house, ever!"

Irene Coleman leaned over to kiss her daughter on the forehead, got up from Charlene's bed, and said,

"You should get some sleep now, we have to be up for church early."

Charlene nodded her agreement and Irene crossed the room towards the door, opened it as she shut off the lamp by the door, went out in the hallway, then took a few steps towards Ruthie's room. She opened Ruthie's door and saw that the girl had indeed fallen back asleep despite her certainty that Santa Claus himself was downstairs.

Irene looked back towards the open doorway to Charlene's room and thought to herself: This is just like one of those boxing matches that Gerald and the boys listen to on the radio, with Joe Louis or one of those other fighters. Round One was now finished, the initial jabbing and probing of each other's defenses, and Irene and Charlene were heading to their respective corners. Maybe, just maybe, Charlene would throw in the towel and decide that marrying Larry Moncheck sometime over the next few months had indeed been nothing more than a whimsical flight of fantasy, a sixteen-year old girl desperately grasping for a handgrip on adulthood.

But if not, if Charlene persisted in this notion, then they all should watch out for Round Two: Only over Irene Coleman's dead body would her daughter become a sixteen-year old or even seventeen-year old bride to anyone, especially Larry Moncheck.

❀ ❀ ❀

Irene was already in their bedroom when Gerald entered. She wasn't asleep or even lying down in bed, but rather was still fully dressed, sitting on the edge of the bed, appearing to be deep in thought, a lit Pall Mall resting in her right hand.

"Christmas is ruined," she said quietly, looking over towards the door at Gerald.

Gerald's eyes raised and his brow furled; surely he couldn't have heard his wife correctly.

"What?" he asked.

"Ruined," Irene repeated. "Christmas is ruined."

"What are you talking about?" he asked, puzzled.

"What do you mean 'what am I talking about?'" Irene answered him, much of her frustration that had been building since early that evening when Jonathan hadn't showed up on time for dinner bubbling over. "Look at Jonathan; look at Joseph's nose; look at Charlene."

She shook her head.

"Christmas is ruined," she repeated yet again.

"Don't say that!" Gerald snapped at her, catching Irene off-guard; she rarely heard that tone in his voice, and she couldn't remember the last time it had been directed at her.

Suddenly he heard *all* of what Irene had said.

"What's this about Charlene?"

Irene told Gerald what she had learned from Lois Walker, and about the just-concluded confrontation with her daughter. Gerald couldn't believe what he was hearing. Having finally talked himself into believing that the "Jonathan situation" would resolve itself—he would get over the girl, he wouldn't go off half-cocked on Friday and still enlist in the Army anyway—now he had *this* to deal with.

Still, when Irene had finished, he had a hunch that perhaps his wife was making too much out of this whole thing with Charlene and Larry. He tried to imagine the worst—his daughter dropping out of high school to marry Larry just before he headed off to boot camp—but he couldn't even conceive of any images to bring his fears to life.

"We'll see," he said to his wife, "but I think it will all work out OK with her."

"What did he tell you, then?" Irene asked about Jonathan, changing subjects.

"He didn't say, but I think it probably has something to do with her going out with Stan Yablonski's boy last weekend," Gerald lied, keeping the entire truth from Irene yet at the same time giving her some inkling of what that truth was as an explanation for their son's previously unthinkable behavior.

"See? That's what I mean, Christmas is ruined," Irene said once again. "Jonathan's girl does something, Charlene..."

She didn't finish the sentence; tears began to fill her eyes.

"I just wanted to have one last Christmas for the entire family," Irene said, her voice remaining even despite the tears. She crushed out the cigarette in the ashtray, too discouraged to continue to smoke.

"And we still will," Gerald said softly, sitting down on the bed to the left of his wife much as she had sat down on Charlene's bed next to her daughter only a little while before. "Like I said, Jonathan is home safely, he's not feeling too great but he'll be OK. Charlene is still here; it's not like she ran off with Larry to elope. And the other children are just the same as they were. They're all here, *we're* all here, and it's not even 1:30 yet; most of Christmas is still ahead of us, right?"

More tears in Irene's eyes, but she nodded skeptically.

"Look," Gerald said tenderly, "we better get used to things turning out not like we expect them to be. With everything that's going on so far in the war..."

He hesitated before continuing.

"We just have to start taking things day by day, especially after the boys go off to the war," Gerald said quietly. "We did it for so long during the Depression, we can keep doing it while the war's on. I know you had your mind around this Christmas being a certain way but with the war and all, things are suddenly a little different for everyone. But we have to look at the good things; like I said, Jonathan is home, he's safe, and he'll be OK. You'll wake up in a few hours and he'll be in his room, he'll go to church with the rest of us, open presents with the rest of us, and have holiday dinner with everyone else. The same with Charlene, right?"

"I guess," Irene said skeptically.

"So even if he's sad," Gerald said, "at least he's alive. Thank God that we're not Karol and Margaret Rzepecki, waiting this very moment for Paul's body to get shipped back home, going through all of Christmas Day still in mourning for him, right?"

Irene looked over at Gerald.

"You're right," Irene said softly.

Gerald reached out with his right arm, placing it around his wife's shoulders and pulling her towards him. Irene melted into her husband as fresh tears flowed.

"We'll just take everything one day at a time," Gerald said again. "This is the first Christmas of the war, and I don't know how many more there will be, but we'll just be thankful for whatever God chooses to bless us with and try not to curse him for whatever might befall us. And so far, right now, we're all still all right; let's just be thankful for that."

Irene just nodded her head that was buried against her husband's right shoulder, desperately trying to believe him.

And they were all right, for now; the entire family. At least five of them were particularly tired at 7:00 that Christmas morning when everyone began to filter out of the bedrooms and down the stairs, straight for the Christmas tree. Ruthie, the first one down the stairs, immediately saw her bicycle with its big pink bow tied to the seat, and began jumping up and down, gleefully clapping her hands. Charlene was the next one down the stairs, walking over next to her sister and saying,

"Wow, Ruthie! Look what Santa brought you!"

"I heard him last night," Ruthie answered, "that's why he needed to bring a helper with him down the chimney, to get the bike in here!"

"That's right," Charlene agreed, turning at the sound of footsteps to see Jonathan and Thomas coming down together, followed shortly afterwards by Joseph. There was almost no visible evidence of the trauma to Joseph's nose—despite the blood, Jonathan apparently hadn't hit him hard enough in the wrong place to do any damage. All five of the Coleman children began pawing through the gift-wrapped packages, looking at the names written on the tags for their own names, excitedly guessing what each package might contain. In the midst of it all, Irene Coleman came down next, catching Charlene's eyes when the girl again looked back towards the stairs at the sound of footsteps, their eyes telling each other that for the rest of the day, at least, the truce they had reached in the wee hours of the morning would remain in effect.

Irene then looked over at Jonathan, who from outer appearances at least seemed none the worse for yesterday's travails. As she reached the bottom of the stairs Jonathan looked back at his mother, locked gazes with her for a few seconds, gave a slight nod—an "I'm OK, Ma, but let's not talk about it" nod—then turned back to rummaging through the presents with his brothers and sisters.

Gerald finally made his way downstairs, the last of the Coleman family, coming to a stop next to Irene at the bottom of the stairs, taking in the scene of his five children excitedly picking up and passing around the gift-wrapped presents. For now, at least, all was well.

The Coleman family tradition had long been that each child could unwrap a single gift before breakfast and before heading to church; the rest of the presents would remain wrapped under the tree until they all returned from St. Michael's, at which time everyone would make short order of the remaining packages.

Ruthie, cunning even in the midst of her rapture over the bicycle, argued that since the bicycle wasn't gift-wrapped it didn't count for "unwrapping purposes" and that she should still be able to unwrap one of her other presents. Irene yielded to the girl's pleas; Ruthie certainly had enough other packages under the tree that there would be plenty for her to unwrap after church anyway. The agreement, though, was that Ruthie would go last among the five children since in a way she had also gone first, given that she was now fondling the cool pink-colored metal of her bicycle.

The traditional order had always been youngest to oldest, so Thomas went next, selecting the package that when unwrapped revealed his new Rawlings baseball glove. "Wow!" was all he could say, but his eyes said the rest; pure joy.

Next came Charlene, who selected a small package that turned out to contain a small cultured pearl necklace that Irene had purchased at Horne's.

"I hope you like it," Irene said to her daughter.

"Oh, I do," Charlene said, and she did, her mind involuntarily conjuring images of Larry squiring her to a restaurant or nightclub, the pearls clasped around her throat.

Joseph, suspecting that one of his packages of the same dimensions as that which contained Thomas' baseball glove might indeed hold the same gift for him, selected a package that when opened contained the handmade winter boots with his father's hallmark craftsmanship. Another gleeful "Wow!" filled the Coleman dining room as Joseph could already feel the warmth of his feet inside the boots no matter how cold it would be outside or how much snow he'd be trudging through.

Next up was Jonathan, who was showing no signs of yesterday's trauma. He selected a package that he was almost certain contained clothing, and he was right: three heavy denim work shirts (his mind quickly flashed to the similarity between the shirts and the utility uniform worn by enlisted Navy seamen, but Jonathan forced the thought away) that would be perfect for the cold winter mornings working for Old Man Weisberg.

"Can I go now?" Ruthie asked excitedly.

"OK, it's your turn again," Irene said, watching the girl make a beeline for a package that (after Ruthie quickly shredded the wrapping paper) contained a wooden doll's playhouse that Charlene had bought for her little sister.

"I got that for you," Charlene said. "Do you like it?"

"I *love* it!" Ruthie exclaimed, bounding towards her sister and crashing into Charlene's legs, offering a big hug of thanks.

"You go now, Mommy," Ruthie turned to her mother and said.

Irene shook her head.

"No, your father and I will wait until we get back from church to open all of our gifts," Irene reminded the children of The Way Things Were Done, but they weren't having any of that.

"Come on, it's a special year," Charlene said. At first Irene thought her daughter was not-so-subtly making some type of statement, but her mind quickly concluded that Charlene meant nothing special (or devious) by her words. This *was* a special year, after all.

The rest of the children all joined in with various versions of "come on, open a present" until Irene conceded, reaching for a package that she was fairly certain was from Ruthie (picked out with Charlene's help). She opened it to find a wallet, something she desperately needed since hers was falling apart; no wonder, Gerald had bought that wallet for her in 1931, ten years earlier.

"I picked that out, Mommy," Ruthie said.

"It's beautiful," Irene said, reaching to pick up Ruth and give her a big hug. "Thank you very, very much."

"You go now, Pa," Thomas said. Gerald kneeled down and selected another package that had the markings of being from Ruthie, and found inside a silver-colored cigarette lighter.

"That's so you can light your Pamalls," Ruthie said, hoping that her father would be impressed that she knew the name of the cigarette brand he smoked.

"That's right," he said, reaching to grab his daughter to pick her up for yet another thank-you hug. "It's wonderful, I can use this every time I smoke a Pamall," Gerald said; Christmas morning was not the time to correct a little girl's minor mispronunciation.

Breakfast was a rushed affair, much as supper was the night before, and then Irene hustled everyone upstairs to use the bathroom and get dressed for church. She then marched the family—the *entire* family this morning, unlike the previous evening—out the door. Unlike most other mornings, in which Irene stepped outside to get the newspaper and the milkman's delivery sometime in the early morning hours, she hadn't been outside the house yet, nor had anyone else. They were all surprised that the morning's weather was... pleasant, that was the only way to describe it. The frigid temperatures that Jonathan had braved for so many hours the previous night seemed to have given way to a blast of warmer air, at least in relative terms. No one would confuse this day for a springtime or summer morning, yet the outside temperature was more like one would expect to find on a late October morning rather than late December; mid-autumn, rather than winter.

By the time they reached St. Michael's every single member of the Coleman family was perspiring heavily under the layers of clothing that Irene demanded they wear, and it wasn't until well into the Christmas morning mass that they all had stopped sweating.

Both Gerald and Irene occasionally looked over at Jonathan to see if he was looking around for Francine, wondering what would happen if the two of them came face to face after Mass was concluded. Halfway through the Mass Irene caught Jonathan staring intently towards the front of the church, almost straight ahead, and she followed his gaze and located the back of Francine Donner's head. Suddenly Jonathan's eyes shifted towards his right, catching his mother catching him staring at Francine. They locked eyes for a brief instant, and then he went back to looking at his hymnal.

The Mass was concluded and the Colemans were outside St. Michael's and on their way home minutes before (by Irene's calculation) the Donner family would even reach the back row of seats on their way out. Confrontation avoided; Irene added another post-service thank you to Jesus for taking the time to answer her seemingly insignificant prayer.

❀ ❀ ❀

After returning home, the Colemans made short order of opening the rest of the Christmas gifts. Wrapping paper was ripped, ribbons and bows went flying, and everyone's Christmas bounty was revealed. Irene Coleman got her new bathrobe, along with a new blouse that she hoped she'd have the opportunity to wear out for a restaurant lunch or supper if a little bit of normalcy returned to their lives in the next year.

The boots and football cleats, the coats and school clothes and work clothes, the toys... all of the Coleman children's presents came forth. Irene's Christmas gift to Gerald turned out to be a new fawn-colored felt fedora, replacing his decade-old steel gray one with its frayed hat band and dulled color.

"You'll wear that when you go to work at the war plant," Irene's words suddenly reminding Gerald of yet another disruption to their way of life on top of the previous night's events with Jonathan and Charlene.

"It's wonderful," he said, crossing the dining room to give his wife a quick thank-you peck on her cheek, the most demonstrative he ever was with his affection in front of their children.

Christmas dinner had always been an Irene Coleman specialty, and this year was no exception. Turkey, ham, stuffing, potatoes... all the traditional favorites graced the Coleman table. The dinner chatter was mostly continued discussion about everyone's Christmas presents: how Thomas would no doubt become a football and baseball star with his new glove and football and cleats; how Ruthie couldn't wait for the snow to melt so she could take her bike out, and how the others would all take turns teaching her how to ride it; how Jonathan's work clothes and boots would come in handy starting tomorrow morning when he went back to work.

Just after 3:00, Christmas dinner now concluded after the pumpkin and apple pies had been completely devoured and the children scattered to various parts of the house, Gerald flicked on the radio and searched for a station that was playing Christmas music. No news, Irene had warned him, hoping that a single day might pass without more disheartening news from the war fronts.

No such luck, when the Mutual network followed *Deck the Halls* shortly after 3:30 with:

```
We interrupt this music program for the
following bulletin. Tokyo radio is
reporting that the British Governor of Hong
Kong, Sir Mark Young, has surrendered Hong
Kong unconditionally to the Japanese. The
surrender occurred at...
```

Hands came flying from every corner of the room, all furiously trying to shut off the radio; as if by preventing the Mutual Broadcasting Network's signal from entering the Coleman house this latest terrible news might simply dissolve into nothingness; as if it would simply be occurring in some parallel world like in one of those H.G. Wells or Jules Verne books that the boys occasionally read. Irene Coleman's hand found the switch first, turning off the radio; apparently even this holy day was susceptible to being violated by that terrible war being fought out there.

❀ ❀ ❀

4:20... ironically, exactly the same time to the minute that Jonathan had left the Coleman house 24 hours earlier on his fateful trip to the Donner house.

Jonathan walked over to the coat rack and began putting on his muffler, his gloves, his coat, and his hat. The surprising morning warmth hadn't lasted past early afternoon, and with the sun's descent accelerating the winter bite was back in the air.

"Where are you going?"

Hearing his father's voice Jonathan turned around. He had hoped to simply slip out of the house unannounced, not having to lie to either of his parents about his destination. Still, just in case, he had concocted his story.

"I'm just going for a walk, you know, think things over a little more," he said, trying to put as much conviction into his voice as he could.

"How about some company?" Gerald asked, catching Jonathan off-guard.

"Um... uh... no, that's OK, it's pretty cold outside, you don't have to go out there," Jonathan stuttered.

"Oh, that's all right, I need to get some fresh air," Gerald countered, not being put off.

Oh, shit, Jonathan thought.

"Pa, I really want to think this over myself, OK?"

Gerald wasn't dissuaded.

"Tell you what," he told his son, not breaking stride as he suited up for the winter cold, "let's take a short walk together first; how does that sound?"

Jonathan knew that his father's question wasn't really a question at all, but rather a command.

"I guess," Jonathan answered, not understanding why his father was so insistent on suddenly accompanying him but, more importantly, trying to figure out how he could shake his father as quickly as possible. He had planned on arriving at Donnie Yablonski's house just as darkness fell to give himself the advantage of knowing what was about to happen and Donnie, with as little light as possible, put at a disadvantage... not to mention being caught off-guard with Jonathan suddenly on his doorstep. Jonathan would move as quickly as he had on the Schenley football field and by the time it was all over, Donnie would be lying there in a bloody heap, more dead than alive.

"Let's go."

Gerald's voice brought Jonathan back from the future that would be to the present. He followed his father out the door to the sidewalk, where Gerald turned and began walking in the direction of his shop.

"So I believe you're planning on paying a visit to Donnie Yablonski after all," Gerald said, looking over at Jonathan. Jonathan stopped dead in his tracks but Gerald kept walking for a couple more strides, and then stopped as well.

A look of determination came to Jonathan's face.

"I'm going to do it anyway," he said, eyes suddenly narrowing at his father, shooting the fires of rage even as his voice remained even-keeled. "That son of a bitch did that to me..."

"So you're going to beat the hell out of him and that will make things all better?"

Jonathan shook his head rapidly.

"No, it *won't* make things all better," he said angrily, his tone now matching the look in his eyes, "because things *can't* be all better now. But he deserves that after doing that to me..."

"Jonny," Gerald said quietly, walking towards his son to close the gap between them, "listen to me. What did I tell you last night about keeping your cool? I know that what happened hurt you, and you want to hurt Donnie back. It was a rotten thing he did, but let me tell you, unless he forced himself on her..."—Jonathan's look told Gerald that wasn't the case at all—"then she was partly to blame also, right?"

"I'm just telling you," Gerald continued, "that I know you're angry and hurting and at this very minute it feels to you like a good fight is the way to make things right. Think of it another way, even beyond keeping your cool. You need to save the fight in you for when you will really need it. Store it up; don't waste it on Donnie Yablonski, because someday you might be in the middle of a battle and things will be really tough, and you'll have to call on that fight in you that you didn't waste on him to get you through it, maybe even to keep you alive."

Gerald paused, looking at his son.

"Am I making any sense to you? All I'm trying to say is that you've always been a good, sensible boy. As strong as you are you haven't gone around picking fights with other guys; it's almost as if you've been saving it all up for when you might need it someday. You started to do some fighting last night with the recruiting sergeant and with your brother, but both of those were small potatoes. But if you go over to the Yablonski's and beat the hell out of Donnie, then you'll have wasted everything you've been saving up, and when you're over in the war you might not have that extra fight in you when you really need it."

Jonathan slowly nodded. He didn't quite follow his father's logic, talking about "fight" as if it were something he could touch and store and call on when necessary, like money from his job that he put into his bank account. Still, he did get the main gist of his father's plea to him: don't do this, you'll not only be sorry but someday you may have to pay the ultimate price in exchange for what you are about to do. Coupled with the previous night's—actually, today's early morning—admonition to keep his cool, he could feel his determination to make Donnie pay after all, despite the fight with Joseph last night over exactly that very thing, quickly fade away.

"All right," Jonathan said slowly.

"All right?" Gerald repeated Jonathan's words, this time a question: are you telling me the truth?

"All right," Jonathan confirmed, and Gerald nodded in reply.

Jonathan turned to walk back to the Coleman's gate, but Gerald put a hand on his son's shoulder.

"Let's keep walking, just for a little bit," he said.

Jonathan shrugged and then turned around and again began walking away from the house. They walked around the corner, down the next street, and wound up in front of Gerald's shop. Gerald took off his right glove, reached into the right pocket of his trousers for his key to the store, and then unlocked the door, nodding for Jonathan to precede him inside.

"I have one more Christmas gift for you," Gerald said to his son.

"Oh?" Jonathan replied, expecting to see his father walk over to one of the shelves or open the storage closet and pull out another gift-wrapped package.

Instead, Gerald took off his left glove and reached into his left trouser pocket and then pulled his hand free, reaching across towards Jonathan's right hand, holding out what looked to Jonathan like a silver dollar.

At first Jonathan had the wild thought that his father was giving him a dollar and sending him off to go for coffee and sandwiches, just like when Jonathan was a young boy helping his father in the shop after school. He half expected to hear his father warn "bring me back all the change" as he used to say every time. Jonathan was just about to remind his father that none of the places nearby that would have sandwiches and coffee for sale would be open on Christmas Day.

Then the type of silver dollar caught his eye: an old-fashioned Morgan dollar, the kind that was rarely seen anymore in circulation, and from the deep recesses of his mind he recalled a long-ago story, and knew what his father was doing.

"Take it," Gerald said, handing the 1891 Morgan silver dollar—*his* lucky or magic or blessed silver dollar—to his oldest son, who complied.

"I had planned on giving this to you right before you shipped out, whenever that would be," Gerald said. "I told you that my father gave that to me just as I was shipping out for the Great War," he continued and Jonathan nodded.

"I always thought I'd give this to you either when you went into business for yourself or when you shipped out," Gerald continued, "and I always hoped that it wouldn't be when you were heading off to war. My father never said anything to me but I think he had hoped the same thing, that he'd give it to me when I took over the shop from him, but I headed off to the war first so that's when he gave it to me. With you, when they bombed Pearl Harbor and we got into it I knew that that would be..."

"I want you to have this now," Gerald interrupted himself, "not right before you leave."

Gerald looked as deeply into his son's eyes as he ever had, and ever would.

"I think you need this now, and I want you to have it," he said.

Jonathan's right hand closed over the coin and he nodded, but before he could thank his father Gerald added,

"Keep it in your left pocket, I think for some reason it gives you better luck there."

Another nod from Jonathan, followed by a hug from his father.

"Merry Christmas," Gerald said.

Epilogue—Friday, December 26, 1941

The alarm bell went off at 5:30, but Irene Coleman had already been awake for about fifteen minutes, her mind scheduling and rescheduling and again rescheduling the day's chores and tasks. Yesterday being Christmas, Irene's regular schedule had been thrown for a loop, but Christmas was now over; back to the grocery shopping and dusting and trips to the butcher and baker...

She also thought about the visit yesterday from Larry Moncheck, bringing Charlene's Christmas present to her. Gerald had gone for a walk with Jonathan and hadn't returned yet when Irene heard a knock on the door just before 5:00 that afternoon. She opened the door and, upon seeing Larry standing there, coolly invited him in, calling for Charlene at the same time.

Larry's visit was brief. He gave Charlene his Christmas present—a gold-plated necklace with a tiny diamond in the middle of a heart pendant, which Charlene later showed to her mother as proof that Larry had not gotten her an engagement ring—and Charlene gave him the cufflinks, tie pin, and collar stick that she had bought for him Monday night at Horne's. Irene had left them alone in the living room, hustling Ruthie, Thomas, and Joseph into the kitchen for cups of hot cocoa, and by the time the cocoa had been consumed Larry was gone. Irene didn't learn any more details of his visit from Charlene, not until much later, but after he left she was confident that she wouldn't be the mother of a bride anytime soon, no matter whether Charlene actually did marry Larry someday or not.

Jonathan worked until almost 1:00 that afternoon as the entire crew at J. Weisberg & Sons worked extra-long hours to make up for the warehouse and the store being closed the day before. Old Man Weisberg's sons asked Jonathan how his Christmas was, what kind of gifts he received, and he showed them the sturdy work boots he was wearing that his father had made by hand and the work shirt he was wearing that his parents had bought him. He gave them an abbreviated rundown of the presents his brothers and sisters had received—Ruthie's bicycle got prominent mention—as well as his father's new fedora and his cigarette lighter from Ruthie for his "pamalls."

Jonathan didn't say a word about what had happened with Francine's rejection of his proposal on Christmas Eve and the aftermath. Though it all had happened less than 48 hours ago, the events were already blurring in his memory. Perhaps soon—not today or tomorrow, but sometime not too long afterwards—he would think of Francine Donner dispassionately, as simply an "old girlfriend" without the ache in his heart that was still there when, in an unguarded moment, his mind wandered in that direction. And as for Donnie Yablonski, he was leaving today—he might have already departed on an afternoon train, not too far from where Jonathan stood at this very moment—and as with Francine, someday he'd think of Donnie without anger or hatred. Still, Jonathan would have to fight the urge for some time to come to not wish for Donnie's death or life-altering maiming on some Pacific island or somewhere in Africa or Europe.

Jonathan Coleman mentioned none of this to the Weisberg boys and the other workers who wandered over for a short break of coffee and conversation. He also didn't mention the 1891 Morgan silver dollar. He didn't quite know the words to use to describe the meaning behind the gift and besides, even though his father didn't say so, Jonathan had an overwhelming feeling that whatever "powers" the coin possessed were heightened and strengthened by not speaking of them.

"Go on, get out of here," Old Man Weisberg growled at 1:00 and Jonathan walked up to Penn Avenue, waited for the next streetcar, and went straight home where he remained for the rest of the day.

The day after the first Christmas of the war.

Coming in 2011

The Coleman family saga continues in the second tale in this series of four novels set against Coleman family holidays in the 1940s and then concluding in the late 1970s

Thanksgiving, 1942

Come spend the first Thanksgiving of the war with the Coleman family and the return of the two older sons—Jonathan and Joseph—for a brief leave following basic training... and what all family members expect will be their last Thanksgiving at home for a long while. Halfway across the world their cousin Marty, who has already been to war, is spending his Thanksgiving with his sea-mates on the USS Augusta, thinking about and missing his family back home.

Irene Coleman is determined to make this Thanksgiving as joyous as possible for everyone in her family who will gather around her table and share the holiday festivities, despite the wartime circumstances and how difficult a year 1942 has been on the war front and also the home front. And as happy as Jonathan is to be spending the holiday with his family before his likely departure for combat, he also dreads the inevitable crossing of paths with his would-have-been fiancé Francine Donner since his feelings for her are as strong as ever. Jonathan has spent the entire train trip home wrestling with the question of whether or not he should make another try with Francine, her Christmas-time rendezvous a year earlier with Jonathan's friend Donnie Yablonski that forestalled Jonathan's engagement proposal notwithstanding.

THANKSGIVING, 1942 follows Jonathan, Joseph, Irene and her husband Gerald, and the other members of the Coleman family in the days leading up to the first Thanksgiving of the war.

Want to be notified when **THANKSGIVING, 1942** is available? Visit http://www.alansimonbooks.com to register to be notified when you can purchase the eBook or a print version of the next tale in this captivating four-novel series.

*If you enjoyed **The First Christmas of the War** and can't wait to read **Thanksgiving, 1942**, then while you're waiting you'll also enjoy Alan Simon's novel **Unfinished Business**, set in post-war 1951 Pittsburgh.*

———

Roseanne DeMarco often thought about her brief two-month affair with Frank Donaldson throughout the nearly nine years that followed those summer months of 1942. Almost every time, in addition to slipping into a near-trance as she vividly relived some moment or another during the affair that was burned into her memory, she found herself asking the same question she had asked herself so many times while it had still been going on: Why?

The explanation—the justification—offered by Roseanne's conscience for what had happened in July and August of 1942 was always the same: she simply hadn't felt truly married, with her brand new husband Joey she had suddenly realized she barely knew before he was called away to the Army. And when the suave Frank Donaldson, the cousin of one of her friends, joined the group of young women in a nightclub one evening Roseanne all but forgot that she was a newlywed. The affair abruptly ends after two months when Frank is called away to the Army and at almost the same moment—and quite a surprise and shock to Roseanne—her husband Joey winds up coming home and assigned to guard Pittsburgh's steel industry for the duration of the war.

Flash forward to mid-1951.

After nine years of tranquil (if complacent) marriage to Joey DeMarco and three sons, what would be Roseanne's explanation and justification in the years to come for resuming her affair with Frank when he suddenly reappears in the middle of June that year... only weeks after Roseanne's husband was called back into the Army and sent to fight in the Korean War? And what will be the outcome of this renewed affair when—or if—Roseanne's husband returns from war?